# THE LAST BALL OF SUMMER

## A NOVEL BY STEPHEN BIGNELL
about cricket and the great war

## ENGLAND WILL NEVER BE THE SAME

Grosvenor House
Publishing Limited

The right of Stephen Bignell to be identified as the author of this
work has been asserted in accordance with Section 78
of the Copyright, Designs and Patents Act 1988

The book cover is copyright to Stephen Bignell
Cover images - credit to: VBVVCTND, simon_g and wickerwood

This book is published by
Grosvenor House Publishing Ltd
Link House
140 The Broadway, Tolworth, Surrey, KT6 7HT.
www.grosvenorhousepublishing.co.uk

This book is a work of fiction. Any resemblance to
people or events, past or present, is purely coincidental.

A CIP record for this book
is available from the British Library

ISBN  978-1-83975-940-6

# INTRODUCTION

This story began life as a spoof of those schoolboy *Boy's Own* sporting tales – so enjoyed by wishful young lads in the early days of the 20th century – before developing into a satire of upper-class manners, cricket etiquette, public schools, child abuse and the human waste of war, specifically World War One or The Great War as it is more commonly known.

It is partly based on the true history of Clifton College Public School, whose entire cricket 1st XI volunteered to join the armed services at the outbreak of war in 1914, with the inevitable tragic and poignant consequences.

The story follows the highs and lows of their sporting, and later military, careers, their knockabout and smutty schoolboy humour, not to mention some amorous adventures, but beneath this youthful gaiety lurks something infinitely more sinister.

The 10th (Sportsman's) Battalion of the London Regiment is fictional, though it is doubtless typical of the many 'pals' battalions raised from Lord Kitchener's volunteer citizen armies of 1914 and 1915. The account of the action at Gommecourt, part of the Battle of the Somme, is however true, along with the divisions, brigades and regiments that historically took part.

Wickham Dale College for Boys – the famous private school for aspiring young gentlemen – is fictitious, there being no connection between such incidents described as taking place behind the walls of this institution and any other of the great public schools of England at the time.

Stephen Bignell
London 2021
*Summer's last ball; bowled, batted and run,*
*Scored and recorded, and now there are none.*

# 1 – INNOCENCE
## England 1904

Albion is dreaming, as providence awaits,
Sleepwalking unhurriedly to its fate

JOHN BIGGLESWORTH – *Innocence*

Two children playing, a boy and a girl. The boy is fair, about eight or nine years old, but small for his age. The girl is smaller still, perhaps a year younger. She has big brown eyes and long, dark hair that flows almost to her waist, not shortened since the day she was born. They seem comfortable together, as if they are two halves of the same picture. The boy is quiet, gentle of nature. He is the follower; she is the leader.

He takes great care to make a posy of flowers and twigs, shaped into a crown, which he places softly on the girl's head, as if they are acting out some ancient ceremony. She smiles, then stands on tiptoe and puts her arms around the boy's neck, kissing him gently on the lips because she has seen grown-ups behave this way; she doesn't yet understand the true meaning of such a gesture. The boy pulls a face and wipes his mouth with the back of his hand. The girl purses her lips, as if in anger, but then her face widens into a toothy grin and a girlish giggle.

1

She takes the boy's hand, barely touching, leading him. He feels safe with her. He trusts her, believes in her in an unknowing, childish way, does whatever she asks of him. They walk hand in hand beneath a clear blue sky across a field full of the greens and yellows of a high summer. She leads him towards the nearby woods, the woods their parents have forbidden them to enter. She is not afraid, for she feels safe with this boy. He is her soulmate; she is his. Together they have no fear of the present or the future.

Beyond them, in the wider world, England stands free, blessed with almost 60 years of peace from conflict, the Empire prevailing at the zenith of its power. Settling old differences, Britain and France conclude The Entente Cordiale - not yet a military agreement, though France has one with Russia - each promising aid should the other be threatened by the Central Powers – Austria, Germany and Italy, who renew their own entente, fearing encirclement. Unknown to the future combatants, the battle lines have been drawn.

# 2 – PLAY UP, PLAY UP
# AND PLAY THE GAME

*The sword and the cannon may bring about peace,*
*Where one side or other must fall*
*But to make up at once all bickering's to cease*
*Give me, O give me the bat and the ball.*
An old Cricketer

BRITISH TRENCHES OPPOSITE THE FORTIFIED
VILLAGE OF GOMMECOURT, PICARDY, NORTHERN FRANCE

1 JULY 1916

Captain Freddie Wright-Herbert of Company C, 10th (Sportsman's) Battalion, Royal London Regiment, part of the 56th Division of Britain's Third Army, looked at his watch for the umpteenth time in the past hour. It was 7.15am. All down the line to the south could be heard the relentless clamour of the guns, just as there had been for the past seven days. They were bombarding the German front line in preparation for the 'big push'. Kitchener's great volunteer army was about to fight its first battle.

Freddie and his battalion had been in France for almost a year. He had signed up in 1914 alongside many of his fellow 'Widdlers', the former pupils of Wickham Dale College for Boys. His batman, Corporal Tommy Banter, stood beside him at the bottom of the trench, nervously polishing his

3

rifle. Tommy had been two years below Freddie at the school but had subsequently fallen on hard times after being 'requested to leave'. He had signed up to the regiment as a private soldier; most of his fellow scholars had been commissioned. He had found himself teamed up again with his former house and cricket captain.

'Fifteen minutes to go, Banter. Getting a bit windy?'

'Not me, skip,' chirped Tommy, his heavy tin helmet almost obscuring his pale, gaunt face. 'The Colonel's asked me to stay behind and mind the store.'

'Banter, you are such a wag!' laughed his company commander.

'No, sir, straight up. Unfit for duty. Gammy leg.'

'Ha, ha! Even at a time like this you are still playing the joker.'

Thomas Edward Banter was indeed a joker. To him life had been one long laugh, but at this moment he did not feel much like laughing. His bowels were loosening; there was a nauseous feeling in the pit of his stomach and his mouth felt as parched as the desert. His throat was so dry he was almost choking. Utterly terrified at the thought of going into battle, Tommy was desperately searching his wits for a way out of this situation, though he was reluctant to let his great hero down. He gazed at some of his chums and comrades waiting along the trench, some smoking, some trembling, all with distant, terrified looks on their faces.

'No joke, skip.'

Freddie seemed to drift away for a moment. 'Banter, old chap, you never did tell me why you were sent packing from school. Was it something awful?'

'Case of misunderstanding, sir. I never did what they said I did.'

Before the older man could probe any further, a piercing and unworldly scream broke the tension.

'Good God, what on earth was that? Sounds like some damned popsy fetching off!'

'It's Private Harminston, sir, just back from no man's land with a stretcher party. Word is he's lost both his legs. Shall I give them a hand?'

'Well, that's bally inconvenient. He was due to play in the divisional cricket match next week. We'll have to find another opening bowler now. Poor show.'

Tommy said nothing, unmoved by his captain's lack of feeling. Wright-Herbert sucked deeply on his pipe. Even in this hell hole, Tommy's former head boy looked like a god. He was tall and fair-haired, and well-built with noble features. Tommy had hero-worshipped Freddie from their first meeting, perhaps harbouring feelings that dared not speak their name.

The officer pulled a silver-lined flask from the pocket of his immaculate uniform. 'Fancy a stiffener, old chap?'

'I'd rather have a wheeze on your pipe, skipper.'

'Certainly, young fellow. A couple of puffs on this and you won't even feel the bullets going in. My father brought a hundredweight of the stuff back from India. Down to the last few ounces now.'

Bullets going in! thought Tommy 'But I'm not part of the attack. I've got a chit from the MO,' he gulped, desperately

5

seeking some understanding and compassion in his officer's face.

Freddie fixed the younger soldier with his deep blue eyes, running his finger either side of his yellow moustache. 'Now look, old boy, where I go, you follow. Anyways, need someone to carry the stumps, bats and balls, etc., in case we can get a game over there.'

'I don't think the Germans play cricket,' observed Tommy.

'Damn right they don't. Perhaps if they did, we wouldn't be fighting this bloody war.'

A shell exploded nearby, close enough to make everyone in the trench duck.

'Blasted artillery! Their guns are so far back they're out of our range. We're sitting ducks.'

That did not offer Tommy much solace. He took a few deep drags on Freddie's pipe and handed it back, a huge grin spreading across his face. Briefly, he didn't feel quite so scared.

'Lethal stuff, skip!'

'You know, Banter,' began Freddie, 'this isn't going to be the picnic everyone thinks it'll be. We are the end of the line. Ours is only a diversionary attack to keep the Huns away from the chaps down south. That's where all the big stuff's going in. The likes of you and I, we're bloody expendable!'

'That really is a great comfort to me, sir.' Tommy's gallows humour did little for his bowels, which were getting so loose he would soon have no control over them.'

'Permission to go for a shit, sir?'

'No time for that now.'

'Couldn't I stay behind this time? I'm in a frightful funk.'

Wright-Herbert put a comforting hand on the other man's shoulder. 'We all are, Tommy, but think of it like this. You'd be letting the old school down. Do you know, most of the old cricket XI are nearby? Signed up to a man in 1914. My brother Jimmy is a subaltern in the company occupying the next trench. Jack Bigglesworth and Will Fulton are here, Dangerfield and Renshaw too. Just like in the old days. Never let it be said that a Widdler funked his duty.'

He paused to let Tommy take in the suggestion. 'Remember that day you and I strode out to open the batting for Weston House against Pongo Smelling and his fast bowlers from Gentleman House on a bad wicket? Well, think of that as what we're going to be doing in a few moments' time; strap on our pads and walk out there with our heads proud and our upper lips stiff. That's the way a Weston man does it. You must play this Hun with a straight bat, though he may bowl you a bumper or try and run you out when you back up too far. He's not a gentleman, you see. He doesn't know what cricket is and what it isn't.'

'Are you afraid to die, sir?'

Freddie put a strong hand around Tommy's shoulder and thought deeply. 'If the great umpire gives me out, I shall accept it without demur. After all, anything else just wouldn't be cricket.'

'I'd rather be playing cricket now, sir, even facing Pongo Smelling on a bad wicket can't be as frightening as this.'

Captain Wright-Herbert nodded but remained silent. Puffing fiercely again on his pipe, he pulled out the pocket watch from his uniform and noted the time once more. It was a beautiful morning, he thought, perfect for a game of cricket. Suddenly, as if the mighty god of war had paused for breath, the guns fell ominously silent. Freddie closed his eyes and let out a deep sigh. Momentarily, he was back at Lord's, scoring a century for Wickham Dale in the annual match against Heaton.

Meanwhile, in the rear trenches, Lieutenant Jack Bigglesworth waited patiently. He was part of the second wave of attack. It was a bright, warm morning but he felt himself shivering with fear. After breathing deeply, he took a slug of whisky from a flask then pulled out a small, battered photograph from his top pocket, a picture of a young woman with twinkly eyes and a knowing half-smile. He ran his finger over it gently, as if he were somehow touching her, then shut his eyes and wished he were with her, or anywhere but here.

A massive explosion, somewhere down the line, brought Freddie and Jack back to their senses. A huge underground mine had been blown, the signal to start the attack. Freddie glanced at his watch again and observed it ticking slowly around to 7.30am.

He put his whistle to his lips but had to spit because his mouth was so dry. He had never known fear of this kind, on or off the cricket field. Fear was alien to him anyway, but this was something different. He pursed his lips and blew. This time it worked. The shrill noise, repeated in every few hundred yards of trench, started the attack.

Tommy Banter started humming to himself, then a few quiet words followed:

> I don't want a bayonet in me belly,
> I don't want me bollocks shot away.
> Take me back to dear old Blighty, where
> I can fornicate me bleedin' life away.

He felt himself being lifted physically up the ladder into the open ground. Freddie dragged him to the top of the parapet, his other men following, some cheering but most of them silent.

The battle to end the war had begun.

# 3 – THE LONG FIELD

*A spot more beautiful, the earth could not yield*
*Than our lovely, homely cricket field*

JOHN BIGGLESWORTH – *The Long Field in Summer*

WICKHAM DALE COLLEGE FOR BOYS
FOUR YEARS EARLIER

The Long Field. God's own patch. The celebrated greensward, scene of so many feats of glory, the cricket field of Wickham Dale College sat in a natural hollow with a high bank on one side. The school buildings themselves stood above it on a plateau, raised up from the main road between London and Brighton at the top of a steep hill leading from the main gates. Behind the buildings was the river, on the other side of which stood the boys' dormitories and other facilities, reached by means of an old stone bridge. A low fence and a line of horse chestnut trees separated the Long Field from the other sports fields, which included two overlapping junior cricket pitches in what was known as the Short Field. Further back, behind a low hedge, the rugger and hockey pitches could be found.

Wickham Dale was the third oldest public school in England, having been founded by King Henry VI in 1456, and had a long tradition of sporting excellence. On warm summer days the boys would sit on the bank overlooking the cricket field, eat their lunches and talk of feats past, present and imagined. The Wickham Dale Cricket XI was the pride of England. Once a year they would grace Lord's for their annual contest against Heaton College, one of the social highlights of the cricket calendar, along with the Gentlemen v Players and Oxford v Cambridge fixtures. Eight 'Widdlers' – college old boys – had gone on to play for England at either cricket or rugby. At least a dozen others had become celebrated politicians or decorated war heroes.

There was little doubt that, of the present generation of scholars, Freddie Wright-Herbert would progress to become yet another eminent old boy, if not perhaps the greatest of them all. He was already head boy, captain of the cricket and hockey XIs and the rugger 1st XV, worshipped by his contemporaries as an almost god-like figure. Though academically sound, it would be his sporting prowess that would generate lasting fame. He was a product of two illustrious families – the Yorkshire Wrights, gentleman farmers and landowners from the Middle Ages, and the Essex Herberts, an aristocratic military dynasty originating from the Royal Tudor court.

His celebrity had spread to other theatres, for Freddie's sexual adventures were the stuff of legend. When reputedly not buggering his fags or other junior boys he was wreaking havoc among the female population in the nearby village of Wickhamstead or the salons of London society. The most recent tale to abound, apocryphal or otherwise, concerned a recent 1st XI fixture with Ednesbury School, where he had opened the batting and been 114 not out at luncheon, which he wolfed down in a few minutes before disappearing for a tryst in the woods with one of the catering girls from the village. In his own words he 'diddled her half to death' then posted a school record of 336 not out from a total of 451 and took all 10 Ednesbury wickets for 13 runs before drinking himself into a stupor during the evening.

Even the masters were in awe of Freddie, who was pretty much allowed free rein as regards his education, attending classes when the mood took him without any recourse. He led his own circle of contemporaries, known locally as 'The Hedonics', who included his younger brother Jimmy and cronies Daniel Dangerfield and Sebastian Renshaw. Indeed, Freddie bowed to no one, with the possible exception of Renshaw, a stocky, fun-loving brash fellow, whose family owned half the county of Surrey and who was constantly selected for the 1st XI despite being no more than an average batsman and a mediocre bowler. Quite what hold Sebastian had over Freddie was unclear, but it did not no go unnoticed by his peers.

In addition to being school head boy and other duties, Freddie was also captain of Weston House, whose record in the sporting field had not been good for some years, being perhaps better known for its academic successes. The house captain was determined to turn things around, with special regard to the Wankeen Cup – the inter-house cricket competition.

The designation 'Wankeen' – unsurprisingly the subject of much sniggering among junior boys – had its origins in India, though the actual derivations were obscured by the mists of time. Weston had not won the trophy since 1897 but had qualified for the 1912 final by defeating All Saints House, thanks to another century and five wickets from Freddie. Facing them would be the powerful Gentleman House – named after a previous headmaster, Ebenezer Gentleman. The 'Gents', as they were colloquially known, had a hostile bowling attack and top-class batsmen, and had easily overcome Weston in the previous two seasons of Freddie's watch.

*

The match was due to be played two weeks hence in the Long Field and on that Thursday lunchtime a gaggle of boys were sitting on the bank overlooking the hallowed field.

'We're in big trouble,' said Jack Bigglesworth, a slim, fair-haired serious-looking boy. 'It looks like Stuart-Smith is a non-starter.'

'What does that mean?' asked the impish Tommy Banter, a gangly lad with slick black hair parted down the middle.

'He is in the slough of despond after getting out for a blob in the Saints' match,' answered Jack. 'He says he doesn't want to play anymore.'

'It sounds like he's in a royal funk to me,' said Billy Hill. 'Jolly bad show if you want to know.'

'No one's interested in your opinion, fatty four-eyes,' opined Tommy. 'What's it got to do with you anyway? You won't be taking his place. You're too fat, half-blind and can't run more than 2yds without falling over, ha, ha, ha, ha, ha!'

'Well, that's just where you're wrong, Banterbags,' Billy responded, 'because Freddie said I can play if I bowl well in the nets tonight.'

'Cripes!' gasped Tommy. 'How come you're such a favourite with Freddie suddenly? Have you been offering him your ring? Ha, ha, ha, ha, ha, ha!'

'I'm sure I don't know what you mean by that,' Billy said, blushing 'and even if I did, it wouldn't be true, so go and boil your head!'

'He's one of our best players. We need him,' sighed Jack.

'Who, Billy?' asked Tommy. 'Ha, ha, ha, ha, ha!'

'Stuart-Smith of course,'

'I heard he was caught trying to get into Matron's medicine cupboard. He got a beating from the head,' said Billy.

'Some say he's an opium eater,' mused Jack. 'That's why he's so moody.'

'What does that mean?' asked Billy. 'Is that some sort of tuck?'

'Don't you think about anything except your stomach?' joked Tommy. 'The word is that you'd offer your bottom hole for the price of some tuck, ha, ha, ha, ha, ha!

'I don't understand what he's saying,' moaned Billy,' but it doesn't sound like the sort of thing one chap should be saying to another.'

'Yes, button it, Banter,' broke in Bigglesworth. 'Better still, go and wash your mouth out.'

'Ha, ha, ha, ha, ha, ha!' cackled Tommy.

'Now look, chaps,' said Jack, 'we're supposed to be sorting out the team for the big final, not joshing around.'

'Exactly, but what I don't get is why Freddie isn't doing this himself. He's the bally house captain, for heaven's sake!' It was Calvin Moseley, a big, strapping, menacing looking lad from the fifth form. He had joined the throng on the bank.

'Freddie's busy with school stuff,' answered Bigglesworth, 'so he's delegated it to me, seeing as I'm the only responsible person here.'

'He's right,' said Moseley, 'all the sixth form chaps in our house are swots. There's no one apart from Freddie even half decent at cricket. It's up to us fifth formers to sort this out.'

'Exactly,' confirmed Jack, 'but we're still struggling for even a half-presentable side.'

'Well, I'll have to play I suppose,' said Calvin.

'But you're useless!' broke in Billy. 'You don't know one end of a bat from the other and every time your bowling gets clattered you pretend you've hurt your back.'

Calvin moved aggressively towards Billy, but Jack intervened. 'But he's good at fielding, Billy, and if any of the Gentlemen start getting jolly batey, Calvin will sort them out.'

'You should pick my little brother,' said Calvin, threat averted, 'He scored a 50 in the juniors' game last week and took three wickets.'

'But he's only a second-former,' observed Tommy.

'That may be so,' agreed his brother, 'but he's a big boy for his age and not afraid of the ball.'

'All right then,' agreed Jack. 'Get him to the nets this evening and Freddie can have a look, but those Gent bowlers are fast. I wouldn't want him getting hurt.'

'Don't worry, he won't funk it, Biggles. We Moseleys are made of stern stuff.'

\*

The sun was high in the sky, though a cooling summer breeze blew across the cricket ground, fanning the boys on the bank. Lunchtime was almost over, but few of the students were in the mood to return to class.

'We're still a few players short,' bemoaned Jack.

'There's always that northern oik Duckworth,' pointed out Moseley. 'He's from Yorkshire or some godforsaken place and no one can understand a word he says, but he's dashed keen by all accounts.'

'True, he's a scholarship boy,' agreed Jack, 'but they reckon people from Yorkshire are good at cricket.'

'I say, what about that new Indian boy, Ali Khan or whatever his name is?' suggested Tommy.

'Eeergh! A bloody wog!' cried Billy.

'Yes, well might be a bloody wog, as you so delicately put it, but his father is the Jamshed of Bollowari, or some such bally thing and one of the richest men in the East,' said Calvin, who knew about such things.

'Is there a shed full of jam?' asked Billy expectantly.

'Thinking of your belly again,' observed Tommy. Better hope old Professor Purviss doesn't spot that bag of custard tarts in your desk during English class, or you'll get another bum bashing, ha, ha, ha, ha, ha!'

'Yes, well he won't unless some rotter sneaks on me.'

'Hang on, there's that Australian boy in the lower sixth,' broke in Jack. 'He did quite well in the last game. What was his name?'

'Scott Mackenzie,' said Calvin, who prided himself on knowing the credentials of every boy in school.

'Not another bally colonial!' complained Billy.

'Suffering cats!' exclaimed Tommy. 'You really are full of racial prejudice.'

'Typical working-class chauvinist,' observed Calvin.

'What do you mean "working class"? returned an angry Billy. 'My father's the richest businessman in the midlands.'

'He's a grocer,' said Calvin contemptuously.

'And why do you chaps keep using words I don't understand?' added Billy.

'If you paid attention during English instead of stuffing your face...' Jack's explanation was cut short by the ringing of a bell signalling the return to lessons.

'Look, six o'clock at the nets and don't be late,' instructed Jack, 'and someone remind Will Fulton, if he hasn't got his head still stuck in the latest *Wisden Almanack*.'

# 4 – NET PRACTICE

*He played his cricket on the heath,*
*The pitch was full of bumps.*
*A fast ball hit him in the teeth,*
*The dentist drew his stumps!*

Anon – *Stumps Drawn!*

It was a balmy, still summer's evening as the boys assembled in the corner of the Short Field for practice nets. There were three of them, separated from each other by strong netting, which was pitched beneath the giant chestnut trees that separated the junior pitches from the senior one. Two of the masters, professors Jeremy Brooman and Jeremiah 'Jesse' James, both of whom were keen cricket-watchers, sat on a bench on the top of the bank to ensure there was no misbehaviour.

Jack Bigglesworth, Tommy Banter and Calvin Moseley had arrived early to set things up. In one of the adjacent nets the boys from Gentleman House were doing the same. A new boy came on the scene, small, thin and dark skinned. 'Ah, welcome Ali,' cried Biggles, shaking the boy's wiry hand, which felt cold and clammy in his grasp. 'Chaps, this is Ali the Jamshed. I think we should call him 'Jammy.'

'Yes, I am liking that very much,' said the new boy, grinning broadly.

Just then, Will Fulton came hobbling up. 'Oh, crikey!' cried Tommy. 'Looks like the Willow's crocked again, ha, ha, ha, ha!'

'Oh, no!' groaned Jack. 'That's all we need.'

'Sorry, chaps,' said Will, 'sprained the old ankle again.' He was a tall, lanky boy with fair hair and a cherubic face which masked an amorous nature. 'I say, Matron's got a new assistant. Pretty little thing, straight from school I believe. Looked a proper picture in her new uniform. My little fellow got so puffed up I had to go straight to the citadel and post one off!'

'What is this Sitta Dell?' asked Ali.

'The Citadel is our name for the communal lavatory,' explained Jack. That's it over there behind the tennis courts; the big green brick building.'

'It's where chaps go when they want to be alone,' suggested Calvin.

'And perform acts of frightful beastliness, ha, ha, ha, ha!' added Tommy.

'I am still not understanding,' said Jammy. 'What is 'posting one off'?'

'Erm... er... boy's relaxation, ha, ha, ha!' grinned Tommy.

'Never mind, Jammy,' said Jack, noticing the poor boy still looking puzzled, 'you'll soon get used to things. Anyone seen Billy?'

'Heard he was up before Pervy Purviss for another whacking,' said Will. 'He got caught scoffing custard tarts again in English Lit.'

'Oh, my hat! Not again, ha, ha, ha!' laughed Tommy.

Just at that moment Billy was spotted gingerly plodding down the steps from the main school building, carrying his bat and pads.

'What's up, Podger?' grinned Tommy. 'How many did you get or did old Pervy give you a sticky one instead? Ha, ha, ha!'

'It's no joke,' winced Billy, 'I won't be able to sit down for a week.'

'Well, you shouldn't be such a fat, greedy oaf then,' stated Calvin.

*

If things were not bad enough for Billy already, his nemesis Horatio Harvey-Wynford was warming up in the adjacent net. Noting Billy's arrival, he barracked him with, 'What are you doing here, you tub of lard?'

'Billy's been selected to play for the Weston team in the big final,' lied Jack, as it was no means certain.

'You must be tugging my yardstick!' exclaimed Harvey-Wynford. 'Weston must be scraping the barrel and no mistake.'

'Yes, well we're jolly well going to give your house a good licking next week,' returned Billy. 'You see if we don't.'

'Listen, you spotty spunk rag, you fat, foozling ditherer, you footling, floundering doddering dummy! You couldn't knock the skin off a rice pudding!'

'Nice alliteration, Winnie,' noted Calvin.

But Billy had not had a good day and was in no mood for Winnie's constant bullying insults. 'Yes, well, when I bowl at you, I'm going to knock your stumps flying to kingdom come, and at least I don't have to wear my cap all the time because my hair's all fallen out!'

Harvey-Wynford was extremely sensitive about his baldness, caused by a savage bout of alopecia. He put down his bat and squared up to Billy. Despite being a few inches shorter he was a muscular boy and not someone to pick a fight with. He was the captain of Gentleman House and 1st XI vice-captain, and a fine all-round sportsman, second only in prowess and reputation to his great rival Freddie Wright-Herbert – they were two lions in the same jungle. 'Now look here, you oik,' he blustered. 'My father is the British ambassador to America and yours is a glorified grocer, so don't come the big swell with me!'

'He's not a grocer,' corrected Billy. 'He owns a chain of retail shops all over England and I bet he's richer than your father. What's more, we're going to give you a pasting in the Wankeen Cup and if we don't, I'll... I'll... eat my pants! So there!'

'Well, I shall certainly look forward to that.'

'Look out,' shouted Jack, 'here comes Freddie!'

The school captain had indeed arrived, padded up and ready to bat, accompanied by his brother Jimmy and his cronies Dangerfield and Renshaw. Jimmy wandered over to the next net as he was a member of Gentleman House. Resplendent and looking truly professional in his red, blue and gold 1st XI cap, Freddie marched purposefully to the wicket and took guard. 'Right, who's first then? Let's be having you.'

Now the head boy could be something of a menace in the nets, dancing down the wicket in cavalier fashion and smashing everything back at the bowlers. One boy had been seriously injured in this way; he was too slow to take cover and had his jaw and most of his teeth broken. His family subsequently removed him from the school. Another boy had nearly been brained by Freddie's bowling when he accidently loosed off a head-high beamer. Young Roland Moseley and other juniors were dispatched to the far reaches of the field to retrieve the battered balls.

Freddie was briefly bemused by new-boy Jammy's leg breaks and googlies though soon his deliveries were getting the same treatment. All the while, Billy sat glumly on a nearby bench feeling sorry for himself.

'Come on, Billy,' chided Jack. 'Freddie will never pick you if you don't have a bowl.'

Reluctantly, Billy picked up an old ball and prepared to deliver, Freddie eyeing him up and down with some surprise. He stumbled stiffly to the bowler's stump and sent down a long hop that Freddie pulled so hard that it almost burst through the netting and hit his brother batting alongside.

'I say, steady old boy!' exclaimed Jimmy.

After a few others had their turn again Billy was persuaded to try another ball, he lumbered in a couple of paces and let fly. Whether it landed on a bad piece of turf, or Freddie was expecting another lollipop, the ball cut back sharply, kept low and squeezed between Freddie's flailing bat and his pads, sending the stumps flying.

Now the captain had been bowled out before, when he had become tired or bored, by the likes of Harvey-Wynford and the demon Gentleman quickie Pongo Smelling, but never by a junior boy in a net. As if something had disturbed the universe, the youthful hubbub of the scene slowly quietened, everyone stopping what they were doing and gaping in amazement. No one could recall this happening before.

'Well bowled, young fellow,' grinned Freddie, recovering his composure and reassembling the shattered stumps, then tossing the guilty ball back to his conqueror. 'Let's see you do that again!'

Billy had to wait his turn as the other bowlers had their go but, forgetting his sore bottom and feeling more confident, sent down a quicker ball to Freddie, who came at him with some intent to restore his shattered pride. The ball spat off the turf and caught the captain a painful blow in his unprotected groin, causing him to let out a loud groan and sink to his knees.

'O cripes! O my hat! What have I done!' cried Billy as he rushed to the stricken batsman.

'I'm all right. I'm all right, don't fuss,' wheezed Freddie. 'Now help me up, there's a good chap.'

Billy and Jack carried the fallen Freddie to the nearby bench, but he was clearly in some pain, having been struck in an extremely sensitive spot. 'I think we had better take him to the infirmary,' said Jack. 'Somebody hop off and warn Matron.'

'The rest of you chaps carry on,' ordered the skipper. 'Dangerfield, you bat next. Moseley, you're in charge.'

'God's teeth! I'm dreadfully sorry,' whimpered Billy. 'It was a complete accident.'

'Of course, it was,' Freddie agreed, recovering his demeanour slightly. 'These things happen. Now, Hill, that was very impressive bowling. How would you like to play in the game against the village on Saturday?'

Billy looked dumbstruck. 'Yes, um... of course I would, but I don't want to let the school down. I'm not much of a batsman and a bit of a slowcoach in the field.'

'Don't worry about that,' returned Freddie. 'If that pitch of theirs is as bad as it was last year, a few overs from you and Pongo and it'll be finished in noticeably short order.'

'Gosh! Thanks, skipper, I won't let you down.'

'Of course not, old boy. Now help me over to Matron, there's a good chap.'

# 5 – MATRON'S REMEDIAL TREATMENT

*Ladies have no sense of cricket.*
*A fence to them is but a wicket.*
*Stumps are remnants, bails are pledges,*
*Strokes are seizures and blocks are wedges!*

Anon

Olive Blackwell had been Matron at Wickham Dale for many years. She was the sister of chemistry master 'Inky' Blackwell and was a plump spinster in her mid-forties with thick, black curly hair and a chubby face, a stern yet seemingly kind soul who regarded the boys as a sort of extended family, perhaps the sons she never had. Beneath this benign façade however, there had been rumours of heavy drinking and inappropriate behaviour with some of the more mature students. Nevertheless, she appeared to retain the patronage of the school's senior officials.

Jack and Billy helped Freddie into the small medical room that was the school infirmary.

'What's this, another wounded soldier?' Olive observed seriously. 'You boys and your cricket, such a dangerous game, I don't know.'

'Thanks, chaps,' said Freddie. 'Now toddle off back to practice. Matron will take care of things.'

'So, where does it hurt, young man?' she asked, once the other boys had left the room.

'Cricket ball amidships, bang on the old plums,' confirmed the head boy. 'Knocked the stuffing clean out of me, I can tell you. Brought tears to my eyes.'

'Weren't you wearing one of those thingamajigs, whatever they're called?'

'Abdominal protectors – don't believe in the things,' boasted the school captain. 'Strictly for girls and cissies. Oww!'

'Well, you are a silly boy then.'

\*

The new nursing assistant, Emily Dickens came into the room, a callow, red-haired slip of a girl, no more than 16. She looked shyly at Freddie and blushed.

'Emily, be a good girl and fetch some clean towels from the laundry room,' ordered the older woman, 'then you can pop off home. I'll see to this poor boy.'

'Yes, Matron.'

'Well, hello and ask me home for tea!' exclaimed Freddie as the girl left the room. 'She's a saucy little thing. What happened to Miss Bedwell?'

'You know perfectly well what happened to Miss Bedwell, you wicked boy,' confirmed Matron. 'She had to leave in a hurry. I had a hell of a job hushing up all that scandal. Lucky for you I'm friendly with her mother, otherwise you'd be in a right pickle and no mistake.'

'It wasn't my fault,' explained the boy. 'She was a proper little cock-tickler. All the boys will tell you that.'

'Well, that may be, but you just keep your dirty paws off this one. She's straight from school, green as grass and sweet as apple pie. Now, drop your flannels and let's have a gander at the damage.' Freddie did as he was told. Olive looked him up and down carefully, then remarked 'My my, you are a big boy, aren't you!'

The laundry was a considerable distance from the infirmary, but in her keenness to do well in her first week in the job, Emily hurried back with undue haste. On reaching the medical room she found the door locked and no one about. She was just about to put the towels in the little storeroom next door when Emily thought she heard a muffled noise coming from the medical room, sounding like something metallic, squeaking and knocking against a solid object. Curiosity getting the better of her she quietly tiptoed to the door and listened more closely.

'Oooh, you are such a big boy, Freddie! Oh yes, that's it, all the way in. Oooh, there's a good boy! You are a good boy!'

It sounded like Matron's voice, though slightly distressed. Emily's first thought was to knock on the door, thinking perhaps that Miss Blackwell was being attacked and perhaps in some danger, but then she remembered there was a little window at the top of the storeroom looking into the medical room. Once inside there the sounds were more distinct. Frantically scrambling up on top of some cardboard boxes to get a view through the window, the sight that greeted her eyes made her catch her breath. Freddie was standing behind the little trolley bed with his back to the window, buttocks bared with his cricket whites down at his ankles. He seemed to be grunting and pushing violently. Matron was lying on her back on the trolley bed, which had been pushed up against some filing cabinets, her uniform up around her waist and her fat legs wrapped around Freddie's neck.

'Oh yes, Freddie!' cried the woman. 'Do it for Matron! I'm almost finished off. I'm arriving! I'm arriving! Freddie!'

Emily let out a loud shriek, her face flushing crimson as she peed herself. Then, with a loud crash, the boxes collapsed beneath her and she tumbled to the floor. As her tears flowed, she realised they must have seen or heard her, so she scuttled rapidly out of the building and into the warm summer sunshine, sobbing quietly. Down below, the boys were busy at their cricket, and no one noticed as she ran for home.

'Well, there doesn't appear to be any lasting damage,' said Olive dryly, sitting and adjusting her dress. 'Everything seems to be in working order.'

'A tad tender, but otherwise much better, thanks,' smirked Freddie, pulling up his flannels. 'I shall recommend your treatment to the other boys.'

'Oh no you won't. You keep your lip buttoned even if you can't do the same with your trousers.'

'I say, you don't think that little popsy saw anything, do you?'

'Don't worry,' confirmed Matron, 'you leave her to me.'

*

The next morning the following announcement was pinned up on the school notice board sports section.

SCHOOL XI TO PLAY WICKHAMSTEAD VILLAGE (away)

Saturday 5th July 1912 11.30am start

F.C.A. Wright-Herbert (captain)

H.M.W. Harvey-Winford (vice-captain)

J.A.W. Bigglesworth

J.K.L. Wright-Herbert

S.S. Renshaw

Monsoor Ali Khan

S. Mackenzie

O.K. Heinz (wicket-keeper)

P.S. Smelling

D.K. Dangerfield

W.S. Hill

12th man J.Z. Owen

Officiating umpire – Professor A.J. Brooman
Stumps 7.30pm
F.C.A. Wright-Herbert (capt.)

*

The following morning Emily reported for work at 9 o'clock as usual, though somewhat nervously after the events of the previous evening. Matron was busy at her desk, which was in a small office next to the medical room.

'Is that you, Emily?' she called.

'Yes, Matron,' came the timid reply.

'Come here a moment dear, will you.'

Emily meekly shuffled into the tiny room, her face flushing up again.

'Close the door and sit down,' said Olive matter-of-factly. Emily did as she was told, though could not look the older woman in the face.

'Now, about last night...'

'I wasn't snooping, Matron,' interrupted Emily. 'Honestly, I wasn't!'

'Yes, dear, I think you were.' Emily's face went redder and redder as she stared at the floor. 'Now look, dear, I don't know what you thought you saw or heard...'

'That boy was being beastly to you!' Emily blurted out, rising from her chair.

'Sit down, girl, and listen to me.' Matron's tone no longer seemed friendly. 'Young Freddie is a very naughty boy and he got a jolly good spanking afterwards.' Olive did her best to keep a straight and serious face. 'Now, boys will be boys and I want you to promise me that you won't breathe a word of this to anyone, otherwise we'll both lose our jobs and Freddie will be in very hot water. Now, you don't want that to happen, do you?'

'No, Matron, but...'

Olive got up from her chair and walked round the desk to where Emily had sat down again, close to tears, and put a maternal arm around the girl's shoulder. 'You're incredibly young and don't yet know the wicked ways of the world.'

Emily felt the older woman's tone soften. 'You and I are special, dear. We're the only two women in the school most of the time, apart from the dinner ladies, so sometimes a few of the older boys can't keep their wicked thoughts to themselves and become very naughty, so we must be very careful. Now, if any boy says or does anything to you which you think is improper, then you come and tell me straight away and I'll go and see the headmaster and make sure they are punished most severely, especially that Fulton boy. He's got the face of an angel but knows more than a boy should at his age. Do you understand me, girl?'

'Yes, Matron.' She quite liked Will Fulton and wondered what Matron was really trying to tell her.

'Right then, now run along to the laundry and get the clean sheets for the beds today and we'll say no more about it.'

'Thank you, Matron.'

No sooner had Emily left the room than Olive locked the door behind her, went to the filing cabinet in the corner, pulled out a half-empty bottle of whisky and poured herself a stiff one. After taking a big gulp, she sighed deeply, then laughed to herself. 'Ah, Freddie,' she murmured, 'you *are* a naughty boy.'

Then she thought of Emily. She liked this girl. She had spirit.

# 6 – THE VILLAGE MATCH

*There surely is no sweeter sound,*
*than bat on ball in a cricket ground*

JOHN BIGGLESWORTH – *The Cricket Ground*

History was not Billy Hill's favourite subject. Furthermore, it was a hot, lazy Friday afternoon and the last lesson of the day. The master, Professor Brooman, was busy writing on the blackboard, so Billy took advantage of the situation by opening his desk and hurriedly scoffing the remnants of the chocolate cake left over from lunchtime. Unfortunately, just as he shut the desk lid, Brooman turned back to face his class. Billy swiftly wiped his mouth and bent down low in his seat. Being near the back of the room he was sure the teacher had not seen him.

'Right then, gentlemen,' boomed the professor, 'Disraeli and the Eastern Question. Which of you discerning scholars will kindly render the class a discourse on this subject?'

Billy had a generally pleasant nature, combined with a broad sense of humour, and not being unintelligent, was generally on good terms with most of the masters, but his relationship with Brooman had always been somewhat unpredictable. The professor was an avuncular soul, a portly man with thick glasses and a mop of black hair beneath his mortarboard, and was prone to sudden fits of irascibility, often rising quickly for little apparent reason. Somehow Billy always seemed to rub him up the wrong way.

'Mister Hill, if you would perhaps honour us.'

'Billy's heart sank. 'S-sir?'

'The Eastern Question.'

'Sorry sir, w-what was the question?'

Brooman's jaunty demeanour darkened immediately. Picking up the light wooden cane from his desk, he strode purposefully towards Billy and thundered 'Are you eating, boy?'

'N-No sir.'

'Please, sir,' cried a voice from the front of the class, a weedy specimen with frameless, round spectacles.

'What is it, Worthington?'

Worthington was renowned for being a teacher's nark and was therefore intensely disliked by almost all the other boys. 'Please, sir, Hill's been scoffing chocolate cake all afternoon.'

'Has he now?' the master noted evenly. 'Mister Hill, have you been nourishing yourself in my class?'

'Please, sir. No, sir,' whimpered Billy.

'Don't lie to me, boy,' bellowed Brooman. 'I can see chocolate all around your chubby chops.'

A snigger went around the class. 'Silence! Hold out your hand, boy.'

'Please, sir... owww!' The thin cane came down hard on Billy's upturned palm, sending a shock wave of agony through his whole arm.

'You know full well that eating is not permitted in class.' The master's voice seemed almost sympathetic as he wandered off. 'Let this be a lesson to you all.'

Brooman strode slowly back to his desk, then unexpectantly turned and addressed Billy again, almost as an afterthought. 'I hear you have been selected for the school XI to play the village tomorrow.'

'Yes, sir,' said Billy proudly amid much murmuring from his classmates.

'A most startling and unanticipated promotion,' observed the master. 'I do sincerely hope you will not let the college down.'

'I'll try not to, sir.'

'However, Mister Hill,' the professor grasped his gown firmly with his left hand and looked Billy square in the face, 'you will be unable to demonstrate your sudden burgeoning talent if you are in detention on Saturday.'

'Oh, sir!'

'You will therefore write me a 500-word composition on Disraeli's administration 1874–1880 and have it on my desk by 10 o'clock tomorrow morning, otherwise I shall sadly have to advise Mister Wright-Herbert of your sudden and unfortunate unavailability for this fixture.'

'But sir...'

'And furthermore, Mister Hill. I must point out that I am also the school's appointed umpire for this fixture, so if you wish me to judge any appeals you should make with equability, then I suggest this piece of work had better meet with my necessary approval by the appointed hour.'

Billy barely understood a word of what his history teacher had said but slumped back in his seat with an air of resignation.

Brooman then marched briskly back to his desk. Worthington stared at him approvingly with a smug grin on his face, which melted rapidly on the teacher's command, 'Hold your hand out, Worthington.'

The startled boy did as he was told, receiving a far more violent blow than Billy. 'What was that for, sir?' he moaned.

'For being a sneak. You have no honour, you wretched boy.'

*

In a state of mounting anxiety, Billy persuaded Jack Bigglesworth, a noted history student, to write the essay for him, though he made meticulously sure to copy it all up in his own handwriting before submission to Professor Brooman. An hour before schedule, at nine in the morning, Billy nervously knocked on his teacher's door and entered on command.

The professor studied the essay carefully as the boy stood opposite him in a cold lather. At least the master was pretending to study it. Despite their occasional antagonism, Brooman was quite fond of the lad and was keen to see him do well.

'Well, Mister Hill,' the history master said after what seemed an interminable time, a serious expression etched across his round face, 'I doubt very much of this is your own work, but you have nevertheless shown some initiative to complete it by the necessary deadline. However, in the circumstances', the professor paused for dramatic effect, somewhat enjoying the encounter, and Billy could feel his knees knocking together, 'I see no reason why you should not join your fellow cricketers in the game today.'

The boy sighed in deep relief, 'Oh, thank you, sir!'

'Nevertheless,' continued Brooman, with as serious a face as he could muster without grinning, 'should I catch you nourishing yourself again during my instruction you will be dispatched to the headmaster in truly short order for six of the best. Do you understand me, boy?'

'Yes, sir, thank you, sir.'

'Right then, off you go, and may you perform to the limits of your ability, which I suspect may not be too difficult for you.'

*

The game against Wickham Dale was the culmination, not to mention the highlight, of the Wickhamstead Village Cricket Club week. They were a side of mixed ability, mostly farmers and labourers, but there had been occasions in the past when their team had been good enough to get the better of the college team. For its part, the school regarded the fixture as something of a social occasion and generally fielded a side containing an association of senior and junior boys. For this game, however, the college team was a solid amalgam of 1st and 2nd XI players, except for Billy, for the very reason that Wickhamstead had been victorious the previous year in somewhat controversial circumstances concerning accusations of bias against their standing umpire.

The old village ground was less than a mile from the school so most of the team, together with any pupils attending as spectators, made the journey on foot. Freddie Wright-Herbert, along with his chums Daniel Dangerfield and Sebastian Renshaw, chose to ride in the latter's new motor vehicle.

A group of fifth-year boys, comprising Jack Bigglesworth, Tommy Banter, Calvin Moseley and Billy Hill, were marching briskly along the track to the village in the early morning sunshine when the older boys' car came hurtling along at some pace, tooting loudly and causing the juniors to hop smartly onto the grass verge.

'Out of the way, you oiks!' shouted Dangerfield, a somewhat affected boy with a permanently supercilious expression and a monocle screwed into his left eye.

'View halloo!' bellowed the stentorian Renshaw as the car passed, still hooting. He was waving a bottle of champagne around, clearly in high spirits even at this hour.

'Bally prefects!' moaned Calvin. 'They think they can behave just as they like. Someone should teach them some manners. Look at the state they're in and it's not even 11 o'clock yet!'

'Yes, they never take this match seriously,' said Jack. 'It's just one glorified bean feast to them.'

'Well, I hope the wicket's better than the cabbage patch we played on last year,' said Calvin. 'It was like a minefield. Pongo Smelling nearly killed their vicar last year. Got him full on the noddle with a half-pitcher!'

'Probably didn't feel a thing,' joked Tommy. 'These yokels have got pretty thick skulls, ha, ha, ha, ha, ha!'

'Don't be so patronising,' replied Calvin. 'They may be lower class agricultural workers but in their own way they contribute to the national economy and have the same rights as the more privileged minority.'

'Oooh! Hark at him!' cooed Tommy. 'I do believe he's turning into Karl Marx, ha, ha, ha, ha, ha!'

By the time the boys reached the cricket ground on the outskirts of the village the day was becoming quite hot. Being a Saturday, it seemed the whole population had turned out, with bunting and tents all around the ground, despite it not being much more than a farmer's field with a rickety old pavilion in one corner. The ring was well populated with boys from the school sitting on the grass with their packed lunches, fraternising with the locals, especially the bevy of young village girls who always turned out on these occasions.

'Cor, what a spectacle!' exclaimed Billy. 'I do hope they have a good lunch and tea here.'

'Thinking of your fat belly again,' said Jack. 'Lunch is outside the Cock and Bull Inn across the road, usually roast beef, lashings of roast potatoes, Yorkshire pudding and beans, followed by spotted dick and custard, washed down with gallons of ginger beer and lemonade, but we can't have proper beer like the village team.'

Billy's lips were drooling already. 'What about tea then?'

'Tea in the pavilion,' confirmed Jack. 'Sandwiches, cake and orange juice, but only for the boys that are playing.'

'Scrummy!' cried Billy.

'We're off for a good view,' said Calvin. 'Good luck, you chaps.'

Jack and Billy went off to join the rest of the boys getting changed in the old pavilion. Freddie and his entourage, together with Horatio Harvey-Winford, were chatting in the corner, Winnie gaily smoking a cigar, Renshaw and Dangerfield polishing off the dregs of the champagne bottle.

'Tally ho, oiks have arrived!' cried Dangerfield.

'View Halloo!' boomed Renshaw. 'Any more grog?'

Billy felt somewhat bashful in their company and quietly changed into his cricket whites. Freddie sidled over and sat down beside him. 'Here, old chap, you'd better have this.' Billy was handed a bright new cap with red, blue and gold bands. The house caps were also red and blue – the school colours – but each of the houses had a different third band to distinguish its members. Only the 1st XI's had gold bands.

'Gosh, thanks, Freddie!' gushed Billy. 'I thought a chap could only wear one of these if he played for the 1st XI.'

'Well, this is the Big School team, isn't it,' said the skipper. 'I'll try and get you on to bowl as soon as poss, circumstances allowing.'

'Thanks.' Billy gazed proudly at the smart new cap.

'Better see if it fits you, now your head's getting so big.' It was the familiar voice of Harvey-Winford from across the room. Stiffening, Billy put the cap on his head. It fitted perfectly.

'I think we'll bat first if we win the toss,' said Freddie, 'before the pitch gets too dicky.'

*

Freddie did win the toss, sending in his brother and the Australian Mackenzie to open. The village began the bowling with their skipper, the Reverend Golightly, who was a friendly undemanding trundler, and a sprightly looking young left-armer. But with a bumpy pitch and grassy outfield, attack was the best policy, and, chancing their arms, the batsmen rattled up 50 in no time, adding to the carnival atmosphere of the day. A few other bowlers were tried but runs continued to come quickly on the small ground, and despite losing a couple of wickets the school were well placed at 124-2 at lunch, Dangerfield and Harvey-Winford at the crease.

Billy wolfed down his dinner, remarking that it was the best tuck he had eaten all summer and secretly hoping he would not be required to bat, even though he was earmarked for the number 11 spot in the order. He need not have worried, even though the village team introduced their late-arriving fast bowler immediately after lunch.

Gabriel Oakman, the local blacksmith, a huge, fiercely hirsute man with rippling muscles, soon made inroads into the school batting, getting the ball to rise awkwardly from the worn wicket. He struck Winnie a nasty blow on the hip, forcing him to retire from the field, but Freddie, entering the fray at four wickets down, soon got the measure of him, thrashing 54 not out and declaring the innings 45 minutes before tea at 224-7, by which time Pongo Smelling and Danny Dangerfield had reduced the village to 44-5.

Freddie Wright-Herbert was clearly becoming bored with the contest at the village ground, as he often did when the game was too easy for him. During the afternoon he had spotted Polly Plunkett among the spectators – the popsy he had 'diddled half to death' during the Ednesbury match some weeks earlier. Among her various occupations around the village, Polly was a barmaid at the Cock and Bull Inn where her father was the landlord. She was a strapping lass, with rosy cheeks, plump breasts and a shock of blonde hair. Freddie was smitten. 'I say, Winnie,' he instructed his vice-captain during the tea interval, 'take over will you, there's a good chap. Got a bit of a niggle. Don't want to aggravate it with Lord's coming up. Make sure young Hill gets a few overs.'

'No problem, Freddie,' beamed Harvey-Winford, happy at last to be given an opportunity to carry out what he believed to be his rightful duties.

'Aye, aye, totty alert!' quipped Renshaw. 'He's got a niggle all right, in his trousers!'

'Oh, sausages!' moaned Billy as Winnie led the school team out onto the field after tea, 12th man Taffy Owen replacing the absent skipper. 'I'll never get a bowl now.' The vice-captain had been in a foul temper ever since getting the nasty blow when batting and having to retire hurt on his way to a 50. Despite the pain in his hip, he immediately brought himself on to bowl, claiming a wicket with his third ball.

It appeared the game would soon be wrapped up, but in strode Oakman, heavy beard bristling, buttocks rippling and bat twirling. He was a sunbeaten fellow with a thick thatch of hair and was quite an intimidating sight for the bowler, though Winnie knew him of old and had often been his match. Not a man to die wondering, the batsman immediately dispatched his first delivery back over the bowler's head for four. The next ball suffered the same fate, causing Winnie to teapot stiffly, hands on hips, and get a little steamed up. The next ball was dug in shorter and quicker. Oakman tried a repeat stroke, but the ball hit high on the bat and spiralled up in the air in the direction of deep square leg, to the part of the boundary where Billy was grazing and chatting to his classmates.

'Look out, Fatty, here comes a catch!' shouted Tommy Banter.

'Catch it, man!' yelled Harvey-Winford.

At first, the fielder thought the ball was going over the boundary for six, but it had flown too high and was losing momentum, falling out of the clear blue sky straight to where Billy was standing. 'Oh, no!' he croaked, the early evening sun in his eyes. Lumbering forward, he stretched out his arms to where he thought the ball was going to fall, but missed it completely, tumbling over in an undignified heap, the ball landing safely and dribbling over the rope for four runs.

'You blithering, bumbling, blundering bumbucket!' came Winnie's inevitable response to the disaster, hands on hips once more. Billy wished the ground could have swallowed him up. He had dropped a sitter in front of all his friends and the villagers were hooting loudly. 'Go and field longstop!' ordered the stand-in captain. 'In fact, you are such a ditherer you can field there both ends!' Poor Billy was too embarrassed to complain, mewling an apology and dutifully having to puff from one end of the field to the other at the end of every over.

Sadly, for Winnie, things went from bad to worse. Wickets were still falling at the other end, but Oakman continued to wreak carnage, hitting the vice-captain for three sixes in one over, one mighty blow sailing over the pavilion into the next field. By now the bowler was in such a foul mood that he had gone as red as a beetroot, his bowling average ruined and his reputation in tatters. He roared out to Billy to replace him for the next over and retired to the outfield to sulk.

But before Billy got the chance to bowl at Oakman, something he was now dreading, the match was over. Pongo Smelling was back on at the other end and immediately dismissed last man Reverend Golightly, sending all three stumps flying as the batsman backed away to the leg side.

The school had won by 102 runs, but Billy cut a sad figure as he trudged back to the pavilion as the crowd applauded his team. 'That Harvey-Winford is an absolute stinker, if you want to know,' he moaned to Jack. 'I didn't get a bat or a bowl. So much for my school debut.'

'I didn't get much of a go either,' agreed Jack, 'but he's not such a bad fellow really, 'just gets bundled up a bit too much in his own performance.'

'Well, it's a jolly rotten swizz, and where's Freddie when he's needed? Chasing some woman around the woods I shouldn't wonder.'

'Never mind,' consoled Jack, 'it's the house final next week. Freddie's bound to pick you for that. You can get your own back then.'

The two boys showered and changed, though the water was cold as always, then joined their pals for the walk back to school as the sun slowly set on a lovely summer's day. The older boys were permitted to stay on and share some beers with the villagers. Freddie reappeared with a ragged-looking Polly and along with Danny and Sebastian got back so late that the school gates were closed; they had to bunk in over the wall, not for the first time.

There had been better days.

# 7 – STICKY WICKETS

*All the lady folks, love my little strokes*
*When I'm batting on a sticky wicket*
*That's wet as wet can be*
*O my, O my, O my, O me!*

GEORGE GRIMSBY (variety hall entertainer)

Olive Blackwell grunted and sat up in her bed, pulling up the sheets around her bouncy breasts and reaching for her cigarettes. By her side the school headmaster, Alistair 'Stinker' Hughes, let out a satisfied sigh.

'That was an exceptionally gratifying coital episode,' observed Hughes, a well-built, bronzed man with thinning hair. He was a particularly humourless and pedantic Scot in his mid-forties.

'Is that what it was?' replied Olive drily, lighting her cigarette.

'Smoking in bed is a most obnoxious habit,' complained the head.

'So is wearing your mortarboard while we're doing the business.'

'I must do so, as technically I am still on duty.'

'Is that so?' sniffed Matron, reaching for a small whisky flask on the bedside table. 'Fancy a snifter?'

'Miss Blackwell,' stated Hughes with a distinct air of disapproval, 'you know perfectly well I do not partake of alcoholic spirit, never have done and hope I never shall. Furthermore, I desire that you have your drinking habits under better control, as on myriad occasions I have detected a distilled odour on your breath during school hours. This is totally unacceptable.'

'Do you have to be so formal?' she grumbled, 'Can't you call me Olive after all this time?'

'Miss Blackwell, I cannot appear to be over familiar with the staff.'

'Over familiar!' laughed Olive. 'You can't get much more familiar than fucking someone!'

'Matron!' gasped the head, sitting up with a start. 'Such profanity! Kindly desist from that kind of language. It is most unacceptable for a lady in such a responsible position. It is my most fervent wish that you never imprecate in this manner before the students!'

'Then I'm no lady, Alistair, as you very well know.'

'No, you most certainly are not, which is why I can relish our soirees in your cottage of an evening, while Mrs Hughes is at her Women's Institute meetings, without the slightest feeling of remorse.'

'If only she knew what a hypocrite you are,' giggled Olive, taking a swig of whisky.

'As you must be aware,' pointed out the headmaster, 'I have not been permitted sexual congress with Mrs Hughes for many years, due to her feminine condition. I am a vigorous man, which is why I find the necessity to frequent your boudoir. Do not forget, Miss Blackwell, that you owe your continuing position at the school to my constant patronage, ever since that unfortunate incident with the fourth-form boys a while back.'

'It was only a bit of fun. Boys will be boys.'

'It may only have been "a bit of fun" to you, my dear, but there would have been a frightful furore had it not been for my prompt and needful intervention.'

Olive sniffed again, belched and screwed up her face, gazing at her erstwhile lover. Despite his age, he was in good shape, and she did so enjoy their little trysts while the boys were busy practising their cricket. She had been a lonely woman since her old mother had died and was glad of a man to warm her bed occasionally, even if it was a stiff, dreary old stick like Alistair.

'Now, Miss Blackwell,' he said, leaning over and caressing her hair, 'I am feeling especially vibrant tonight, so kindly extinguish that cigarette, reassume your reclinate position and it's all aboard for another trip on the roller coaster.'

'Oh Headmaster,' giggled Olive, 'you are such a romantic!'

*

However, for once the boys were not at their cricket practice, due to the unseasonable heat. Instead, Jack Bigglesworth was busy chairing a selection meeting in the fifth-form common room.

'Right, everyone here? So, let's begin. Weston House team to play Gentleman House in the Wankeen Cup Final on Saturday. Most important match for years, I think you'll all agree.'

'Well, I'm fit now, Biggles,' confirmed Will Fulton, briefly looking up from studying his Wisden Cricket Almanac.

'That's a good start, now...'

'I say,' broke in Tommy Banter, 'did you know that Matron and Headmaster are, er, friends?'

'What do you mean, "friends"?' asked Calvin Moseley.

'He doesn't know what he means,' suggested Billy Hill. 'He's just being enigmatic as usual.'

'He's right,' added Will, 'I saw him going into her cottage last night and he was in there a jolly long time.'

'Probably school business,' said Jack. 'Now, can we get on?'

'Funny business more like, ha, ha, ha, ha!' guffawed Tommy.

'Now, Freddie's skip obviously,' broke in Jack, 'Danny as 2-i-c, then Rickshaw I suppose.'

'Rickshaw's useless!' cried Tommy. 'He bowls pies and bats like a girl, ha, ha, ha, ha!'

'Just like you then!' cried a voice from the back of the room. It was that of Milton Maudling, a tubby, morose boy who had been Weston's regular wicketkeeper until he broke all his fingers. 'At least he doesn't knock his own stumps over trying to play a shot.'

'Oh, I think there's a bit more to Rickshaw than that,' suggested Jack. 'He's a bit unorthodox, but not a bad hitter.'

'And he gets jolly batey if he doesn't get a bowl or bat higher than number six,' added Will.

'I hear Matron and Stinker have tea every Saturday afternoon while we're playing cricket', broke in Tommy, steering the conversation back to his original subject.

'What's that got to do with the house XI?' moaned Jack, getting slightly irritated.

'And then go upstairs to her bedroom.'

'Does having tea make them tired then?' asked Billy.

'No, you goose,' continued Tommy, 'to play mothers and fathers, ha, ha, ha, ha, ha!'

'Clive Searle of the lower sixth says Matron goes down quicker than the Titanic,' added Will.

'That's not funny,' observed Calvin, 'All those poor people drowning in that freezing water. Bad show.'

'Going down where?' asked Billy. 'Where's Matron going down to then?'

'Gavin Rich said she performed an act on fellatio on him,' advised Will.

'Who?' What?

'Matron.'

'Is that some sort of medical procedure?' asked Billy.

'Er... you might say that' grinned Will.

'Felli whatsit?' asked Tommy.

'Look, if we can please get back to the cricket!' broke in an exasperated Jack. 'That's what we're here for.'

'You bunch of turnips!' trumpeted Will. 'There are other uses for your little chap than posting one off or having a piddle! Don't any of you pay attention during biology lessons, the bits about rabbits and their reproductive organs?'

Silence.

'So,' started up Jack once again, 'Scotty can play, then there's...'

'What other uses, ha, ha, ha, ha?' interrupted Tommy yet again, playing devil's advocate.

'It's called sexual intercourse,' continued Will, putting down his Wisden and adopting a serious, adult pose. He was a more worldly boy than the others and knew of such things. 'To procreate, the male must insert his penis into the female's vagina, then there's a lot of pushing and shoving, grunting and moaning, before the male ejects his sperm into the woman. It goes for a swim up some duct or other and fertilises her eggs, then, hey presto, nine months later out pops a sprog!'

Brief silence again, followed by some nervous coughing. Jack and Billy felt their faces flush.

'Yes, well,' continued Jack, regaining some composure, 'now we must have Jammy and Moseley Minor...'

'So, how long does all this take then?' asked Tommy, back on his own conversational thread.

'Oh, just a few minutes, I believe,' confirmed Will, 'Sometimes longer.'

'Hang about,' observed Billy, 'if all that messy business only lasts a few minutes why does it take nine months before the sprog arrives?'

'Ooh, you silly children! I give up!' Will buried his head in the Wisden again.

'I thought intercourse was talking to each other,' said Calvin. 'Is that really how babies are made then?'

'Well, it sounds a dirty, mucky business to me,' said Billy. 'I definitely won't be doing any of that.'

'So how do you know all this then?' asked Jack, giving up temporarily on the selection procedure.

'My sister's a nurse,' replied Will. 'She's also a suffragette.'

'I've got a sister,' chuckled Tommy, 'and she makes me suffer, ha, ha, ha, ha!'

'Oh, my ribs are aching so much,' added Will, 'Someone call Matron and the chest doctor.'

'Frightful beastliness if you ask me!' guffawed Tommy. 'I'd rather have a good buggering from Freddie or old Pervy Perviss, ha, ha, ha, ha, ha!'

'That's just what you'll get if you don't be quiet!' shouted Jack. 'Now can we please get on with the meeting.'

'Old Billy knows all about that,' said Tommy, then immediately realising he might have said the wrong thing.

'All about what?'

'You're always in old Pervy's room. Does he make you bend over so he can have a dicky-back ride, ha, ha, ha, ha, ha!'

The room sensed that perhaps Tommy had gone too far this time.

'Stop it, you rotters!' yelled Billy. 'I don't know what you're talking about!'

'Gentlemen, please!' cried Jack, trying to restore order yet again.

'Come off it,' Tommy was on his bike now, 'everyone knows you've got a juicy little ring, ha, ha, ha, ha, ha!' Poor Billy could take no more joshing and ran from the room in tears.

'My grandfather was buggered senseless at Heaton and he went on to become chancellor of the exchequer,' Will stated, matter-of-factly. 'It's nothing if not character building.'

'That's not funny,' said Calvin. 'It's a bad business.'

'Well, I hope you're satisfied now,' moaned Jack as Billy left the room. 'You really are a bunch of insensitive bounders!'

'Ha, ha, ha, ha, ha! Calm down, Biggles.'

'Anyhow, I think we've finally cracked it,' sighed Jack, 'so here goes – Freddie, Danny, Rickshaw, Scotty, Moseley Major, Moseley Minor, Banterbags, Billy, Willow, Jammy and, finally, yours truly. That should do it.'

'Well done, Biggles. What about Harry Twelfthers?' asked Calvin.

'Ah, how about the scholarship oik Duckworth? He should do it if he's not digging up coal or racing his pigeons.'

'Or eating black puddings, ha, ha, ha, ha!'

'There's going to be a war anyway. A war to end all wars,' piped up Maudling from the back of the room, putting his usual dampener on proceedings. 'My father's a general. He knows these things.'

'Yes, but it won't start before Saturday, will it?' came back Jack.

'He's right,' agreed Calvin. 'The Balkans are a tinderbox now. When it blows it's going to engulf the whole of Europe.'

'It's the French and the Germans,' continued Maudling. 'They hate each other, always have. The Ottoman and Hapsburg empires are on the point of collapse, as is Russia. The French are allied to Russia and to Britain. If a European war breaks out, we won't be able to keep out of it.'

'Wow! Thanks for the history lesson,' said Tommy.

'Nonsense!' blasted Jack. 'What's any of this got to do with us? Our politicians will keep us out of it, and we've got the Royal Navy to keep us safe.'

'Rule Britannia, Britannia rules the waves, ha, ha, ha, ha!' sang Tommy.

'Oh, do be quiet!' complained Calvin. 'Imperialist jingoistic claptrap! The proletariat will rise all over Europe and these backward countries will be introduced to proper socialist democracy. More power to the working class!'

'Oh crickey! Karl Marx is on his soapbox again, ha, ha, ha, ha!'

'You can snigger, Banter, but you and your over-privileged class will be the first for the chop, just you wait and see.'

'Even old Brooman thinks there will be a war,' piped up Will, 'and he should know.'

The room went quiet again. 'Yes, well, the only war we're interested in will be Saturday's clash with the Gents,' Jack pointed out. 'I'll get the OK from Freddie for our team and we can meet up again tomorrow for some last-minute practice. I can't wait for Saturday.'

'Me neither,' agreed Calvin. 'Someone had better go and find Fatty and tell him we were only ribbing. He's not usually so thin-skinned.'

'I think we may have struck a raw nerve, all that business with Pervy,' said Jack. 'He does seem to spend a lot of time in that man's study. Perhaps we should stop ragging him about it.'

'He hasn't said anything, has he?' asked Calvin. 'I mean, if he's being singled out unnecessarily, for whatever is going on, perhaps we should have a word with Freddie.'

'Leave it to me,' said Jack. 'In the meantime, we need to concentrate our thoughts on the match.'

'Maudling's right about the war though,' came in Will. 'I think it wouldn't be a bad idea if we all joined the Officers' Training Corps.'

'What, all that marching up and down and pointing rifles?' returned Jack. 'Personally, I think it's a waste of time. Our army and navy should be able to deal with any eventualities. They are the best in the world, then there's always the Empire. I don't see the need for the likes of us to get involved.'

'I'm not so sure,' Will replied, putting on his adult, serious face once again. If it comes to a scrap with Germany, they've a huge army and will be more than a match for us and the Frogs.'

Jack mused for a bit, then said, 'Well, hopefully nothing will come of it. Let's stick to cricket for the time being.'

'There's an OTC training session after school tomorrow,' Will advised. 'Why don't you come along. It can be quite fun sometimes.'

'Isn't it a bit like being in the Boy Scouts?' asked Calvin.

'A little, I suppose,' agreed Will, 'but you learn about proper weapons and how to lead a group of chaps and so on. Why don't you both give it a try. You never know when it might come in handy.'

'I'm a pacifist,' stated Calvin firmly. 'War is immoral.'

'I used to play soldiers when I was little,' reminisced Jack.

'This isn't playing, Jack. I really think there's a war coming.'

# 8 – THE WANKEEN CUP

*The boys will play until the sun goes down,*
*On our wondrous cricket ground*

JOHN BIGGLESWORTH – *The Cricket Ground*

On Friday the weather broke, and it rained most of the day, huge stair rods of water that created massive puddles everywhere. Consequently, the cricketers were mostly in a state of deep depression, particularly Billy, whose concentration in class wandered more than usual as he kept gazing out of the window murmuring 'It looks a bit brighter over there.' It seemed certain the house final would be postponed, or worse still cancelled altogether. Fortunately, the downpours relented in the evening and Saturday dawned dry if somewhat overcast. The match would go ahead as planned.

'I say chaps, I don't like the look of this,' remarked Jack Bigglesworth as the boys made their way to the splendid new pavilion at the back of the Long Field. 'The wicket could be a real sticky dog if the sun comes out.'

'Best bat first then?' suggested Billy.

'I don't know what Freddie will do if he wins the toss. I wouldn't want to be facing Pongo Smelling if the wicket is misbehaving,' observed Jack.

'Soiling your britches already, phwar, phwar!' laughed Sebastian Renshaw, resplendent in a straw boater.

'He better not,' joked Tommy Banter. 'He bet Harvey-Winford he'd eat his own pants if we lose, ha, ha, ha, ha, ha!'

'Oh, shooting stars,' gulped Billy. 'I'd forgotten about that!'

'You can be sure Winnie won't have forgotten,' said Renshaw.

*

The two umpires walked out to the middle to inspect the wicket, which had not been protected from the weather. They were the respective games masters for each house, professors Brooman for Weston and James for Gentleman. French teacher 'Jesse' James was pushing 70 and more of a hindrance than a help to the cricket fraternity, since he frequently dozed when umpiring, until awoken by a loud appeal, following which he would generally raise his finger and give the batsman out. On the other hand, Brooman was a very impartial arbiter and could usually be relied upon to give an unbiased decision.

Jesse was giving his usual boring lecture to the players in the dressing room about fair play and the spirit of the competition when Freddie Wright-Herbert stumbled in with his cricket bag and slumped down on a bench.

'Oh dear, skipper looks a bit the worse for wear,' noted Jack.

'Out on the tiles in the village again last night,' said Renshaw, 'jabbing that saucy little popsy I shouldn't wonder, phwar, phwar!'

'She's hardly little,' observed Daniel Dangerfield sarcastically.' Boobies like pink cannonballs and thighs like tree trunks, what, what!'

'Buxom is the word,' said Renshaw.

'Wright-Herbert Major!' barked Jesse James, pleased to see his opposition captain not appearing particularly bright eyed and bushy tailed. 'You are not looking your Sunday best, my boy. Not indisposed, are we?'

'It's Saturday,' moaned Freddie. 'Anyone seen the pitch?'

'Bit of a dog, what?' chortled Dangerfield. 'Never mind, let's have a taste of it.'

'That was last night, ho, ho, ho!' boomed Sebastian.

'Ready for the toss, old boy?' Harvey-Winford poked his head around the door, fully changed and looking ultra-smart in his striped cap and white choker.

Wearily, Freddie dragged himself to his feet and disappeared out into the middle with the Gentleman House skipper. This was always a tense moment, especially for each side's opening batsmen. In Weston's case, nobody yet had any idea what the batting order might be. A few moments later Freddie returned looking gloomy. 'I've lost the toss and we're batting. Sorry, chaps. Biggles and Scotty opening please, if you wouldn't mind.'

Jack's heart sank and the butterflies began to flutter in his stomach. The thought of facing Pongo Smelling and Winnie on that pitch filled him with dread. He hurried to the lavatory.

So, it proved to be. The game began with the ring well populated with boys, mostly on the high bank overlooking the ground and many noisily cheering for their respective houses. Winnie seemed to spend an eternity setting the field as Jack prepared for the first ball from Smelling, his bat tapping nervously on the ground and heart thumping away in his chest. The bowler, never one for needing a warm-up, came steaming in, arms twirling, puffing and blowing like an express train, disconcertingly delivering the ball off the wrong foot. He let loose a straight ball on a good length. Jack prodded feebly at it, but it spat off the moist wicket catching the shoulder of his bat and looping up towards the slip cordon behind the wicket. Jack thought he was a goner, but the pace of the ball saved him, just clearing second slip and dropping safely to the ground.

'C'mon, mate!' yelled Mackenzie, and the batsmen ran through for a single.

'O cripes!' moaned Billy from the boundary. 'I definitely don't like the look of this!'

Jack was happy to get to the other end and allow the more self-assured Australian to take on Pongo. Mackenzie was a confident boy who never took a backward step and played Smelling with some courage. Jack was happy to face the more accurate but less dangerous Harvey-Winford. The tall Australian stroked a couple of effortless boundaries, evoking much whooping from the ring of spectators, but then succumbed to an absolute snorter from Pongo which eluded his forward stroke and sent his middle stump cartwheeling back some 20yds.

'Oh Khartoum!' cried Renshaw, the next man in.

'Rickshaw won't last long out there,' observed Calvin as the outgoing batsman slowly returned to the pavilion shaking his head. He was proved right as, though not lacking physical courage, the new man was all at sea against top-class quick bowling, his unorthodox style better suited to slower deliveries. In the very next over he dollied up Winnie to cover point: Weston House 11-2. Freddie should have been next man in but was in such a state of lethargy that he had still not changed into his cricket whites, so Will Fulton marched boldly out to bat in his place.

'We need to dig in for a while,' ordered Jack as he met the new batsman at the wicket. He was a plodder at the best of times but on a pitch such as this he merely concentrated his mind on pure survival.

Will's survival lasted just three balls. He was a gangly left-hander, employed limited foot movement and simply swung his bat at everything. After a couple of futile swishes at Winnie the next ball demolished his stumps. Freddie was still faffing about so Mansoor Ali Khan the Indian prince came in next. He was so short and wiry there appeared to be nothing of him, but he was full of confidence and played some wristy strokes straight from the off, mostly on the leg side.

'Look, it's Ranjitsinhji, ha, ha, ha, ha!' cried Tommy Banter. 'We'll be all right now.'

At the end of one tough hour of play the score stood at 47 for 3, with Jack having scored just seven. The atmosphere was now quite humid with another storm threatening and the damp ball was swinging about considerably and coming off the wicket at different heights.

'Come on, Biggles, stick in there!' encouraged Billy from the safety of the pavilion. Jack was determined to do just that, but the flamboyant Jammy soon met his downfall. Winnie had rung the changes and brought his spinner on to bowl, who immediately tempted the young Indian to mistime a long hop straight into the hands of deep mid-wicket.

Finally, Freddie entered the fray, still looking a bit fagged, but Jack was aware that even a half-awake captain was more than a match for most bowlers. 'Well done, Bigglesworth,' he droned on arrival at the crease. 'Just keep your end up and leave the rest to me.'

The Gentleman House captain immediately recalled Smelling for another spell, but the sun was out now and the pitch had become strangely placid. After a couple of fidgety overs, Freddie got his eye in and began clumping the bowlers to all areas with some disdain. Although the field became more spread out, he advised Jack that he didn't fancy running any quick singles, so proceeded to score in boundaries or not at all, which annoyed Winnie no end. After lecturing his team for sloppy fielding, he put down a simple catch himself from Jack at mid-on after juggling the ball for several seconds, much to the amusement of Billy Hill.

The Weston team were feeling more confident now and sat back to enjoy the fun. Winnie was tea-potting a good deal and wondering how to break the stand when Freddie's brother Jimmy sidled up to him, holding the ball which he had just fielded. He had no great love for his elder sibling, whom he felt received all the plaudits and attention; he reasoned that he was just as talented but that he went largely uncredited. 'Look, Winnie,' he whispered, 'Jesse's dozing off again. The next time Freddie gets hit on the pads let's all appeal.'

Jimmy was right. The old master was looking a bit dreamy in the heat as the clock ticked around to the lunch interval.

'Wizard wheeze, Jimbo!' agreed the Gent captain as the two players parted.

Jack, standing at the non-striker's end could see something was up. 'Watch out, Freddie,' he warned his skipper.

Winnie was a true sportsman, though not above a spot of sharp practice if the situation demanded, and immediately brought himself back on to bowl for the last over before the interval at Jesse's end. Freddie, feeling somewhat weary and in need of a break, flailed at the first ball and was struck high on the leg.

'Howzaaatt!' yelled Winnie in concert with his close fielders. At first the umpire did not respond, then slowly blinked his eyes, peered towards the other end of the pitch and slowly raised his finger. There was an audible groan from the Weston team and supporters, but much whooping and back-slapping out in the middle. Freddie was dumbstruck. He glared at the umpire, then the pitch and his bat, before slowly turning and walking off.

Lunch was taken with the scoreboard showing 91-5 – Last Man 36.

*

'We're in a spot of bother now and no mistake,' observed Will Fulton as the boys took their places at the dining table for their cold meat and salad. Freddie sat slumped across the table, head on hands and a distant expression on his face.

'That was jolly rotten luck,' commiserated Jack in the captain's direction. 'That ball was going miles down the leg side.'

'Old Jesse needs a new pair of glasses,' suggested Calvin, munching a piece of lettuce.

'He needs to be put out to grass,' said Will.

'Never mind, skipper, got to see the funny side of it, ha, ha, ha, ha!' joked Tommy Banter.

'Fetch off!' bawled Freddie, violently rising from his chair and knocking over some cups.

'Ooops, Freddie's in a proper wax!' exclaimed Renshaw, somewhat stating the obvious.

'Yes, why don't you button it, Banter!' sneered Danny Dangerfield. 'You really are an insensitive little blighter. One should learn the art of diplomacy, what?'

The rest of lunch continued in almost total silence. Freddie had vanished and was nowhere to be seen. 'It's not like him to sulk,' said Jack. 'Something must be up.'

'You're right,' said Billy. 'I've never seen him like this before.'

'Perhaps that Polly popsy has given him the brush,' suggested Will.

'Or given him something else, ha, ha, ha, ha!' suggested Tommy.

'Now listen, Bigglesworth,' barked Dangerfield as he padded up to bat next. 'We're in a bit of a pickle, so it's down to me to get us out of it. I need your best support.'

'OK, Danny, I'll do my best.'

'It's Mister Dangerfield, you junior oik. Your best support, mind.'

'He's a proper snotty-nosed cad and no mistake,' said Billy as Dangerfield disappeared from the dressing room. 'Some

63

of these senior boys think they are God Almighty and need taking down a peg or two.'

'Yes, but it won't be from the likes of us, will it?' stated Jack. 'Meanwhile, I've got to dig a trench and hold the fort for a spell,' he added, mixing his metaphors. 'Danny's not such a bad chap really. It's just his manner. He got Calvin off a thrashing the other day after getting into a scrap defending his little brother, who was being bullied. Then he straightened it out with Freddie when Willow was late for practice.'

'Well, I still think he's a bounder,' said Billy. 'You always think the best of everyone, Jack. You have too generous a nature. It will be the downfall of you.'

'Very philosophical,' Jack was briefly surprised at his pal's sudden profundity. 'You may be right, but now we have to score some more runs.'

Alas, all Jack's promises were in vain. His concentration diluted by a good lunch and 40 minutes' rest, he fell leg before wicket in the very first over after the resumption, having scored 24 in the previous session. Dangerfield fared little better. He was a good batsman but something of a showman and following a brace of cultured boundaries got carried away and holed out to long-on.

Young Roland Moseley, shrouded by the youthful gown of invincibility, showed no fear of the bowling and hit out boldly, once even smiting Jimmy Wright-Herbert back over his head for six, but after accumulating a brisk 14 runs he chanced his arm once too often and was castled by the same bowler. The tailenders – Tommy, Calvin and Billy – offered minimal resistance, though Billy did manage a couple of lucky edges through the slips and a very professional-looking leg glance. An amusing incident occurred when Tommy spectacularly demolished his own wicket attempting a late cut. Renshaw collapsed in a fit of hysterics and even Tommy saw the funny side of it. Some vital runs were scraped together, but the final total of 133 all out was disappointing.

'Come on chaps, we can still win this!' boomed Renshaw during the changeover between innings, especially if Freddie gets cracking. He still looks in a fearful bate!'

# 9 – A GRIPPING CLIMAX

*Fierce came the globe, fizzing thru' the air*
*Whence will it fall, I know not where!*

JOHN BIGGLESWORTH – *The Lonely Fielder*

It was by now a very pleasant, if somewhat humid afternoon. High up on the bank Matron sat serenely in her deckchair, like a queen bee surveying her hive. From time to time, she glanced up from the book she was reading to ensure everything was as it should be. Though technically on duty, in case of an unexpected accident to any of her boys on the field, she felt warm and relaxed. Young Emily Dickens sat quietly beside her.

Just then the headmaster wandered by, doing the rounds with his assistant, the physics master Professor Langstone, a pencil-thin man with a thick moustache and something of a stoop. As she looked up and spotted the head, Olive's heart skipped a beat.

'Good day, Matron.'

'Headmaster. Professor.'

'And a very pleasant day it is too.'

'Indeed'. The lovers were socially awkward outside of her bedroom.

'I trust you are well, Matron?'

'Full of the joys of spring, Headmaster.'

'Excellent, though I must point out it is now high summer.'

'I was speaking metaphorically, Headmaster.'

'Indeed. Though perhaps not meteorologically, or perhaps metaphysically, ahem!' Alistair smiled at his own joke.

'Very amusing, Headmaster,' replied Olive dryly. Trying to be funny really doesn't suit you, she thought to herself.

'Thank you, Matron. I trust Miss Dickens is enjoying the game.'

'Yes, thank you, Headmaster,' gushed Emily, blushing slightly and surprised at the head's attention. Hughes turned and meandered off, Langstone dutifully following in his wake.

'Silly old fool,' murmured Olive, loud enough to cause Emily to giggle. 'Are you enjoying the match, dear?' she said to her assistant after a short pause.

'Ooh yes, I love cricket! My father sometimes plays for the village team.'

'Does he indeed,' said Matron, somewhat absently. 'That's nice.' After another little pause she asked, 'So have any of the cricketers taken your fancy then?'

'Oh yes, that little chap with the white choker.'

'What... you don't mean that Harvey-Winford boy?' Olive's expression was quizzical. 'Oh no, dear, he's far too stuffy.'

'Well, I like him. I think he's cute and cuddly, and very muscular, isn't he?' Emily stifled a grin.

Olive gave her young assistant a puzzled look. 'Do you now? I think he's a bit out of your league, dear.' She paused again for a while, gazing back at her book, but something about this girl bothered her. 'My my, you are coming on a bundle, aren't you? Last week you wouldn't say boo to a goose.'

'I'm learning quickly,' Emily giggled. 'I like that Will Fulton too.'

'Look, I warned you about him. What about that nice polite Bigglesworth boy? He seems steady and dependable.'

'Oh no, he's terribly dull. He was in all morning and hardly hit the ball at all.'

Olive looked at the girl once more. Hmm, I've got a live one here, she thought to herself, then realised she might have been staring at Emily a little longer than was proper.

Emily sensed this and met the older woman's gaze. 'Matron?'

'You're a pretty little thing, aren't you, dear?'

'Am I?' Emily replied pettishly.

'You are going to break a few hearts.'

'I don't think so, Matron. If what I've seen of some of these boys so far, calling themselves young gentlemen, I don't think I'll bother.'

Matron found herself staring again, something stirring inside her soul, something gone and almost forgotten, a memory dark and distant, long buried, murmuring absently, 'She'd be about your age now.'

'Sorry, Matron?'

'Oh nothing, dear, nothing important. Carry on watching the game.' Olive sighed, raised her eyebrows and went back to reading her book, but try as she might, she found it impossible to concentrate on the words in front of her.

*

Back on the field Freddie was indeed still in a frightful wax, choosing to open the bowling himself and charging in like a mad bull. In this mood his bowling could be somewhat erratic, but on this occasion not so, clean bowling both Gentleman openers with less than 10 on the scoreboard. This brought James Wright-Herbert to the wicket. He may not have been in the same batting class as his more celebrated elder brother, but he was determined not to fall victim and dealt with his sibling's thunderbolts proficiently and with some aplomb.

Freddie tired quickly, so brought on Billy Hill at his end. Initially the new bowlers posed few problems to either Jimmy or his partner, the oddly named Oliphant Kendall Heinz. Danny Dangerfield was also approaching the end of his opening spell, with the Gentleman House innings looking comfortably placed at 50-2.

But Jimmy was perhaps becoming overconfident. He stretched for a wide delivery from Billy and edged to the slips, where Jack Bigglesworth took an excellent one-handed diving catch. In strode captain Horatio Harvey-Winford, exuding self-assurance and resplendent in his harlequin cap and white choker, a classical sportsman, perfectly dressed and dapper, a gentleman cricketer in the making. 'Two legs please, Umpire,' he barked confidently. The arbiter duly manoeuvred Winnie's bat into the middle and leg position and the batsman busied himself extravagantly banging his bat into the ground and marking the crease.

Near the pavilion, the disagreeable Worthington, sitting with his equally unpleasant chums, gestured in the direction of Tommy and Calvin, the closest fielders, 'You Weston numbskulls have had it now. Winnie will knock you out in a few overs, ha, ha, ha!'

'Gudday, yer Pommie bastard!' chirped Mackenzie at Winnie from the slips. 'Diggin' a hole to Australia, are you?'

Unused to this sort of disrespectful greeting, the batsman turned around and glared at his tormentor. 'Colonial roughneck,' he muttered.

'Thanks, mate,' returned the Australian, 'Yer lookin' a bit crook today. Not planning to stay long?'

Winnie ignored him, though Billy had a smirk to himself. Distracted by this unwarranted interruption to his opening routine, Winnie inadvertently re-marked his guard a couple of inches to the right of where it had been and slightly too far to the off side, then took up a textbook stance to receive his first ball.

Billy lumbered in and delivered a good length ball on the line of the off stump, which swung in late and eluded the batsman's forward stroke, going behind his pads and clipping the leg bail. For a moment there was disbelieving silence.

'Well bowled, Hillers!' yelled Freddie running in to congratulate the bowler as the fallen batsman tucked his bat under his arm and meandered off slowly shaking his head.

'Bastard took the wrong guard,' laughed Mackenzie. 'Silly bastard!'

One over later the umpires called the tea interval, with the Weston camp now in much better spirits. 'Their two best batters have gone, thanks to Billy,' chirruped Jack.

'Yes, boys, but it's not over yet,' warned Freddie. 'They've still got some decent players to come.'

He was not wrong. Heinz batted steadily to make 37 before being bamboozled by Jammy's leg spin, but in the middle order Sweeney and Buckeridge put on 40 runs with efficacious use of the long handle, particularly to the slower bowlers Ali and Jack. Sweeney, who later went on to fraudulently claim in society that he had played for Surrey, was bold but erratic and prospered with not a little fortune.

By now a weary Billy had been posted to deep square leg on the boundary for a rest, though found little respite as a succession of hits were coming in his direction. Fortunately, the tireless Roland Moseley was posted close by and retrieved many balls meant for Billy, who was fast getting out of puff, his situation not helped by constant chaffing by the horrid Worthington and his Gent House cronies close to where he was fielding.

The afternoon had become overcast again with a hint of warm drizzle in the air, though few spectators noticed much as the match progressed towards its dramatic conclusion. With 20 minutes left before the game was due to finish the batting side had reached 116-7. Freddie was now wide awake, and, assisted by the more tactically aware Dangerfield, shifted his bowlers and fielders about proficiently. Smelling was now at the crease. He was a competent though limited batsman but was sufficiently savvy to farm the strike as late wickets fell. With one over left the tension around the ground was almost unbearable, the ring hushed and expectant. Gentleman House needed two runs to win with one wicket still standing. If they played out a draw the trophy would be retained but Smelling was a positive character and would not settle for a negative denouement.

Freddie took the final over himself, thundering in off a shorter run and hurling down another fast ball, slightly short of a length; the batsmen executed his favourite shot, pulling it high to the leg side and spiralling it into the cloudy sky. With gathering dread, Billy realised the ball was heading directly to where he was fielding. Young Roland started to run towards where he thought it would land, but stopped dead in his tracks when Freddie bellowed, 'Yours, Billy!'

Visons of his previous nightmare from the village match now flashed in Billy's eyes and through his thoughts. If he took the catch Weston would win the match and the cup. If he dropped it – and the batsmen had completed one run and were turning for a second – Gentleman House would win. There was now a deadly silence in the crowd as everybody held their breath in anticipation. During what seemed an eternity the ball was falling to earth. Time seemed to stand still for Billy. He stumbled forward, then back, then forward again, realising it was going to drop in front of him. He fell forward and, amazingly, appeared to grasp the catch just before the ball hit the ground.

A huge cheer went up all round the Long Field as his teammates began to converge to where Billy had fallen full length, but Billy was not celebrating. He scrambled to his feet, making a neutral gesture, casting a glance at umpire Brooman standing close by. 'Please, sir,' he spluttered, 'I think the ball might have hit the ground.'

'Are you sure, boy?' asked the umpire, grimly.

'I think so, sir. I felt the ball hit the ground as I caught it.'

For a moment no one could quite comprehend what had happened. Brooman walked slowly over to Jesse James and spoke to him discreetly. The batsmen, having completed the two runs required for victory, stood together in the middle of the pitch, the whole ground now having gone almost quiet except for a low hubbub.

'What's going on?' asked the Weston skipper as he approached the two umpires.

'It was not a fair catch,' trumped James. 'Your fielder has confirmed it.'

'What do you mean!' thundered Freddie. 'We all saw him catch it.'

'The ball hit the ground,' confirmed Brooman.

Freddie turned to Billy, standing meekly by, a frightened look on his face. 'Well?'

'I didn't catch it fairly,' Billy mewled.

As Freddie stood in shocked disbelief, the umpires spoke to the scorers in the box, where the numbers slowly clicked round to 134-9, confirming Gentleman House had won. The Weston team and supporters, who moments ago had been celebrating, now fell silent. Worthington danced in front of the pavilion, waving two fingers on each hand. Calvin moved threateningly towards him, whereupon Worthington bolted in some haste.

The defeated team clattered disconsolately into their dressing room as the drizzle began to intensify, nobody daring to say a word except for Sebastian Renshaw, the last to enter. Slamming the door fiercely behind him he bellowed at Billy who was cowering in a corner. 'You brainless cretin! Why didn't you claim that catch? You've cost us the cup!'

'Because it wasn't a catch,' whimpered Billy, on the verge of tears.

'No, Sebastian, that won't do!' cried Freddie, 'The boy did the honourable thing and has nothing to reproach himself for.'

'Hear, hear!' cried Jack.

Renshaw could gather no support for his argument, with the inevitable exception of Mackenzie, who growled 'Strewth, you Poms and your sense of fair play!' then stormed out of the room yelling 'Bah!!'

But Billy was inconsolable. In a tender moment, young Roland sat down next to him and patted him on the back. 'It's all my fault!' Billy sobbed.

'No, it isn't,' said Will Fulton. 'Cricket is a team game, and we must all accept responsibility for defeat. At least you got some runs and took some wickets.'

'Absolutely,' agreed Jack. 'It was a fine contest, and we all did our best. We'll beat them next year, just you see.'

*

The players then trooped back outside for the presentation ceremony. Billy wanted to stay inside, but Freddie insisted he take his place with the rest of the team. Although it was still drizzling a huge assembly of boys had crowded around the pavilion to watch. Billy stood throughout with his head hung low, not wishing to meet anyone's gaze. Hardly aware of what was going on, the headmaster's droning voice began to filter through to his consciousness.

'And what a splendid contest it has been, in the finest tradition of our school sports, with the result in dispute right up until the dramatic denouement, with both teams having disported themselves magnificently. Nobody deserved to be downed, but fate decrees there must be victor and vanquished. Both XIs can take intense pride in their performances. However,' he paused for effect, 'the real winner today was the sovran game of cricket itself, the result being commanded by the honesty and fair play of one undaunted boy. We at Wickham Dale pride ourselves on playing our contests with absolute legitimacy and equability, whether in triumph or defeat and, in the words of Kipling, treating both imposters the same.'

Hughes's pompous speech tailed off to a smattering of applause. Only when realising that everyone was looking appreciatively did Billy understand that the head was speaking of him. He looked up see Harvey-Winford proudly holding the cup aloft. He applauded unenthusiastically along with everyone else and was about to turn and return to the pavilion to shower and change when a familiar voice boomed out.

'Just a minute, old chap.' Billy's heart sank again as Winnie strode towards him, but instead of the usual torrent of abuse he was expecting, the Gentleman captain held out his hand. 'Bad luck. That ball that bowled me was a corker.'

Billy timidly offered a weak hand. 'I was lucky.'

'Nonsense, old boy, and you can forget about eating your pants, but don't push your luck next time, eh?'

Winnie strode off to join in the victory celebrations. When Billy looked up again Professor Brooman was standing beside him.

'My boy, that was an honourable thing you did today.'

'I couldn't claim the catch, sir, the ball did hit the ground.'

'I know it did, my boy, and if you had not have owned it, I would have said nothing, but thought less of you. For us Widdlers the playing of the game in a correct and honest fashion is more important than winning or losing. You are a credit to your house and your school. You may have imperfections, young fellow, but you will not fall short of top marks in humanitarianism. I can be assured of that.'

'Thank you, sir,' sniffed Billy, despite barely understanding a word of what the master had said. The empty feeling inside him would not go away, though.

He was still inconsolable in the dorm that night but perked up when Jack reminded him of the trip to Lord's the following week for the annual Wickham Dale versus Heaton match. The whole school had been allowed to skip classes and attend.

# 10 – AN INVITATION TO LORD'S

*Then there's Lord's with its crowded pavilion*
*'Well fielded', 'well bowled', and 'well played'*
*The chaff when the wide is delivered*
*And cheers when a good hit is made*

Anon – *Then There's Lord's…*

The social and sporting highlight of the summer was the Heaton versus Wickham Dale cricket match at Lord's Cricket Ground in St John's Wood, London. The fixture was played over two days at the end of July, shortly before the school broke up for the summer holidays. As a special treat, all those boys who wished to go, could travel up to London by train for the first day of the match. For those selected to play there would be an overnight stay in a swanky hotel.

Billy's mood had improved considerably over the past days, having become something of a school celebrity following his exploits in the house final. He now found students were gazing at him in admiration rather than with the usual disdain. Nevertheless, neither Billy, nor Jack or any of the other fifth formers were selected for the game, which was always a 1st XI prerogative, the only exception being James Wright-Herbert.

Freddie Wright-Herbert naturally captained the team, assisted by Horatio Harvey-Winford as his vice-captain and

Daniel Dangerfield, Peregrine 'Pongo' Smelling, Scott Mackenzie and Sebastian Renshaw, though many wondered how the latter managed to be continually picked for the senior side. Jack, Tommy and Billy and the rest of the fifth year were permitted to attend the first day's play though were instructed to wear their smartest blazers and caps and had to promise to be on their best behaviour throughout.

After the train trip they arrived at the ground early, accompanied by professors Langstone, James, Purviss and Brooman. One hour before the scheduled start the scene was already one of great colour, with Heaton boys milling around, resplendently dressed in their top hats and tails, together with a bevy of smart young ladies parading in the outfield with their summer dresses, hats and parasols. The boys could sit on their own in the free seats at the ground's Nursery End, while the masters took their places among the adults in the pavilion and boxes.

'I say, chaps,' enthused a bubbling Will Fulton, settling into his seat, 'there's some corking fillies about; got my old nose sniffing up already!'

'Well, you better get down to the toilets then and post one off. We don't want you embarrassing yourself, ha, ha, ha, ha!', chuckled Tommy Banter.

'Look, Tommy,' said Jack Bigglesworth at his most profound, 'you must behave yourself and keep your voice down otherwise we'll all be packed off back to school. Everyone in the ground can hear you.'

'Oh, shut up, Jack!' griped Billy Hill. 'Don't be such a wet blanket. Just relax and enjoy yourself. You'll disappear up your own bottom hole one of these days.'

'Yes, if I've told you once, I've told you a million times, don't exaggerate, ha, ha, ha, ha!' chortled Tommy.

'Oh, very amusing, and somewhat clever for you,' said Will. Just then a particularly attractive young woman walked past. She was dressed in pink lace and had a matching hat and parasol. 'Look at that popsy!' he gushed. 'I wouldn't mind posting one in her envelope!'

'What does he mean about envelopes?' asked a puzzled Billy but he was cut short by a loud cheer as the field parade began to disperse and the two captains came out of the pavilion to toss for first innings.

'Look, there, Freddie!' bellowed Tommy, jumping up from his seat, 'Come on, Freddie. Up the school. Down with the Heaton toffs!'

'Sit down,' complained Jack, 'you're attracting attention.' A group of Heaton boys, sitting close by, turned towards Tommy and, putting their fingers under their noses, made a quacking noise. Tommy replied by blowing a loud raspberry in their direction. The chaffing continued back and forth for some time until the Heaton team took the field, Wickham Dale having won the toss and elected to bat.

'Let's get some pop,' suggested Billy.

'Didn't you have some with your packed lunch?' asked Jack.

'I drank it all on the train.'

'How about something stronger,' said Calvin, 'to go with the pack of cigars my father gave me at Christmas?'

'Yes, get some bubbly,' said Will. 'You're a big boy and look at least 18.'

The resourceful Moseley was indeed able to requisition a bottle of champagne from the stall behind the stand, which was passed around the boys with some relish, along with Calvin's cigars. Unfortunately, it was not long before the heady wine began to take effect.

'Look, there's a bobby!' cried Billy, as a portly, mature police officer began to patrol the boundary in front of the seating. 'Move out of the way, please. You're blocking our view.'

'Sit down and be quiet,' warned Jack, who was beginning to regret coming, 'You'll get us all into trouble.' The policeman looked in their direction briefly, then wandered away with the air of a man who had seen it all before.

But Billy, puffed by the wine, would not let it be. 'Go and arrest the umpire. He's just given one of our batsmen out!'

The school had indeed lost a man, Mackenzie adjudged leg before wicket. Another wicket quickly followed, which put the Heaton supporters in good humour.

'Look, they're singing their stupid sailing song,' shouted Tommy. 'Sit down you landlubbers, otherwise your boat will sink, ha, ha, ha, ha!'

One particularly tall Heaton boy became tired of Tommy's constant haranguing, got up from his seat and wandered over to where the Weston House group were sitting. 'Stow that racket, you muttonheads,' said the lad with some authority, 'or I'll stuff those silly caps somewhere they won't see the light of day!'

'Go and chew your testicles!' cried Billy, the champagne fuelling his swagger.

An incident was briefly averted by the sound of a huge cheer from the crowd, as new batsman Freddie Wright-Herbert smote an enormous six over mid-wicket. The Heaton bully thought better of it and walked off with some disdain. 'You're going to get a good hiding now Freddie's in, ha, ha, ha, ha!' bawled Tommy.

He was not wrong, as the rest of the day belonged to Freddie and Harvey-Winford who, in glorious sunshine, put up a stand of 200 for the third wicket in just two hours of effortless strokeplay. Meanwhile at the Nursery End the first bottle of champagne had been followed by another, which only served to amplify everyone's noise levels, especially those of Tommy and Billy. Calvin had become increasingly aggressive as the day wore on and the alcohol took effect, culminating in him throwing pieces of food at the Heaton followers, who responded in kind, so much so that the policeman reappeared to calm down the disturbance. 'Now, now, boys, what's all this about? Settle down please, there's good chaps.'

'Go and arrest those boys for wearing silly hats, officer, ha, ha, ha, ha!' cackled Tommy.

'Is that a bottle of champagne you are drinking?'

'Please, sir,' bleated Jack, 'We're all old enough.'

'Are you now?' The policeman was looking serious and gazed at Billy. 'Is that a cigar you have? Are you old enough to be smoking?'

'Yes, thank you,' burped Billy.

Just at that moment Professor Brooman appeared. 'Is there a problem, Constable?'

'Oh cripes, now we're for it!' moaned Jack, cringing in his seat. He had not been indulging in the festivities and was beginning to feel distinctly uncomfortable at the behaviour of his chums.

'The boys are getting a little boisterous, sir', observed the policeman.

'Don't worry, officer, I'll deal with this.'

'Very well, sir. We don't want any trouble.'

The scene provoked a good deal of hooting from the Heaton section, some of whom were waving their arms and putting fingers under their noses again and squeaking in a desultory fashion.

'Settle down please, boys, and enjoy the cricket,' said Brooman with an unexpected air of calm, before walking away and chatting quietly to the policeman.

'Balaklava, that was a close call!' gasped Will.

'Capitalist lackey!' barked Calvin in the officer's direction.

'Old Brooman's aware it's the end of term,' explained Jack. 'He knows we're only letting off a bit of steam, but just take it easy, will you.'

It was fortunate that the master was now out of sight, for almost immediately Billy keeled over and was violently sick over Calvin's trousers, while Will began coughing violently on his cigar. Nearby, the Heaton mob were laughing and cooing louder than ever. Jack, who totally disapproved of smoking, drinking and any immature behaviour, did his best to calm matters. 'Take it easy, chaps, or they'll be proper trouble in a moment.'

But Tommy was now laughing so much he had almost fallen off this seat. He clutched his stomach and spluttered, 'Heaton boys play with their todgers all night, O ha, ha, O ha, ha, ha, ha, ha!' The whole section of seats at the Nursery End was now staring and wondering what the commotion was.

The big Heaton boy who had confronted them earlier rose to his feet once more and walked up the gangway towards where Tommy was rolling about in his seat and convulsing with laughter. 'You Widdlers are an absolute disgrace!' he hollered with a snooty air. 'You are all a bunch of prissy girls and if you don't shut your portholes, I'm going to punch you all on the nose!'

'Oooh ha, ha, ha, ha, ha, ha, my stomach is hurting!' guffawed Tommy, almost doubled up.

Never one to back down from a confrontation, Calvin squared up to the Heaton boy who spat 'You're all drunk! I've a good mind to go and find one of your masters and report you.'

'I'm terribly sorry,' apologised Jack, 'some of...'

'Go and suck your lollipop, top hat!' interrupted Will.

'Yes, hoppit you stuck up toff!' cried Calvin, moving threateningly towards the boy, 'or I'm going to give you a damned good thrashing!'

Outnumbered and somewhat intimidated, the boy backed away, just as another huge roar went up from the crowd. Freddie had reached his century with a blistering cover drive. All the Widdlers in the ground were on their feet, applauding and waving their caps.

'Freddie! Freddie! Freddie! Hurrah for Freddie and Wickham Dale, rah, rah, rah!' yelled Tommy, falling over Billy, who was retching again. 'Ha, ha, ha, ha, ha, ha, ha. Your ship has sunk! Ha, ha, ha, ha, O my stars!'

Not long after, Harvey-Winford also reached a chanceless century. Freddie declared at the tea interval with the score at 307-5.

'Fancy an ice cream, anyone?' asked Jack as, thankfully, things calmed down in the interval.

'I don't feel very well,' groaned Billy. 'It must have been something I ate.'

'Looks like everything you ate,' quipped Will.

'Better take him down to the boys' room,' said Calvin. 'He's ruined my britches as well as his own.'

The remains of the day were something of an anti-climax. Jack suggested everyone should drink plenty of water and suck sweets, otherwise the masters would discover that the boys had been drinking and smoking. Billy spent the rest of the afternoon asleep or feeling ill, while everyone else quietened down and ate what remained of their packed sandwiches for tea.

Pongo Smelling came out all guns blazing when Heaton batted, knocking over two batsmen with barely a run on the board. The next pair recovered somewhat but by 6 o'clock it had clouded over and was beginning to spit with rain, and the umpires reluctantly led the players off the field.

The boys reconvened with their tutors by the Tavern Stand for the trip home. Billy was swaying slightly and caught the eye of his tormentor, Professor Perviss. 'What's the matter with you, boy!' boomed the master.

'Please, sir,' interjected Jack, 'he's not feeling very well. Food poisoning, I should think.'

'Food poisoning, is it? Report to my study at 9 o'clock tomorrow,' ordered Perviss. Billy's heart sank.

The trip home on the train made Jack feel even more uncomfortable. The group had a compartment to themselves but there were no corridors or toilets, so Billy had to pull down the window and vomit out of the moving train, while Calvin opened one of the doors and urinated, spraying the windows of the next carriage. Jack sat in the corner with a look of scorn on his face, impatient for the journey to end and refusing to offer any comment on the awful behaviour of his friends. Fortunately, they reached the school grounds without further incident.

*

After the day's cricket had ended, the players, along with some of the masters, went to the Park Inn Hotel in the Edgware Road for dinner while professors Perviss and Langstone accompanied the spectating pupils back to the school. After their meal some of the party made trips to the opera or theatre, while others gathered for a convivial evening in the hotel lounge. Freddie Wright-Herbert, Daniel Dangerfield and Sebastian Renshaw formed their usual cabal in one corner, smoked cigars and drank champagne.

'I say, chaps, what, what?' sneered the sarcastic Dangerfield, 'that arse rag Banter requested that he might join us in the Hedonics.'

'What an oik!' barked Renshaw. 'He wasn't serious, was he? I hope you gave him short shrift.'

'Quite so,' confirmed Dangerfield,' a boy renowned for his acerbic wit. 'I pointed out that it took something quite *sui generis* to penetrate Freddie's intimate circle, what, what? I think that flummoxed him.'

'Not many have done that, ho, ho, ho!' cackled Renshaw.

'Indeed,' agreed Dangerfield, 'Freddie's intimate circle is well known for being impenetrable, what?'

'As far as I am aware you are the only one, Sebastian,' observed Freddie drily, finishing off another bottle of champagne.

'What about that oik Banter?' asked Renshaw.' Where did he come from? It's rumoured his father was a blackguard who made a lot of money swindling innocent people.'

'I heard he was the product of some duke, born the wrong side of the blanket,' said Freddie.

'Whatever, he's definitely not one of us, what, what?'

'How about a proper smoke?' suggested Freddie. 'I've got some bhang upstairs. Pater brought a pile back from India on his last visit.'

'Top hole!' exclaimed Danny. 'I'm all for that, what, what?'

'Away to bed, boys?' asked the headmaster, seeing the chums leaving the room. He and his fellow masters had dressed formally in their evening suits.

'Prayer meeting actually,' stated Freddie. 'Chaps need a spot of spiritual guidance before the game tomorrow, then it's off to bed early, if you'll excuse us.'

'Not at all,' replied Hughes. 'Very commendable. 'I was unaware you boys fraternised the Christian Society.'

'Never miss a convocation, sir.' added Renshaw.

'Well, Professor Brooman,' said the head, 'it's very warming to see the boys taking their divinity so seriously.'

'Absolutely, Headmaster,' agreed the history tutor, who had perhaps discerned the true nature of the boys' early departure. 'I must say, Matron is looking very alluring this evening, dressed up as if attending a Buckingham Palace tea party.'

Alistair Hughes coughed nervously as he regarded the school matriarch in all her splendour, sitting on a chaise longue and holding court. She was dressed entirely in black, had a matching hat and veil and was holding a long cigarette holder in one hand and a whisky and soda in the other. Emily Dickens sat demurely beside her, sipping a glass of lemonade and looking distinctly bored.

'I don't quite understand why the ladies have been invited to this function,' mused Brooman.

The headmaster coughed again. 'She is present at my invitation, Jeremy, and has brought the young lady along as companion. Miss Blackwell has little social life nowadays, living alone after the death of her poor mother.'

'Hmm,' observed Brooman. 'I hope she doesn't get too sozzled and let the side down. It would appear she's had quite a few already.' He recalled Renshaw's comment from earlier in the evening, that she looked like 'a tart at a wedding'.

'Fear not,' said Hughes, 'I am keeping a fatherly eye on her.' Shortly afterwards he made his apologies and slipped away to his hotel room. Olive watched him go and shortly after turned to Emily, 'I think it's time for bed, dear. You must be very tired.'

And you must be very drunk, thought her young assistant.

\*

It was past midnight in the hotel room shared by Olive Blackwell and Emily Dickens when the older woman burped and quietly turned on the bedside light to see if her companion was asleep in the adjacent bed. Happy that the girl was in dreamland, Olive put on her nightgown, tiptoed awkwardly to the door and closed it behind her. Luckily, there was no one in the corridor as she stumbled the few yards to a nearby room and knocked on the door. 'Alistair,' she whispered.

'Is that you, Matron?'

'No, it's the bleedin' Queen of Sheba! Who do you think it is? Open the door.'

The door clicked open slowly, revealing the school head dressed in an ankle-length gown and a nightcap.

'Miss Blackwell, kindly keep your voice down. Professor Brooman is in the next room.'

'Oh, he's well out of it. Sleeps like a top. Now, get those things off 'cause I haven't got much time.' The sinful pair tumbled into bed together, Olive giggling like a schoolgirl.

'Oh, Miss Blackwell!' cried Alistair as she smothered him with kisses, 'could you not have brushed your teeth prior to our appointment. Your breath wreaks of alcohol and tobacco!'

'Come on, stop blathering and get cracking. Stick it in. I can't stay too long in case Emily misses me.'

'Miss Blackwell, I am not accustomed to being rushed in my work.'

'Come on, Alistair, let the dog see the rabbit, tee, hee, hee, hee.'

'Matron, you are most inebriated! Get cracking! Stick it in! This is most definitely not language of an amorous nature!'

'Oh, do me a favour!' she cried, pushing the man down on the bed and sitting astride his body. 'I wanna poke, not a perishin' bunch o' flowers!'

'Matron, kindly moderate your language. You sound most workaday!'

'Oh, be quiet, and stop wriggling about, otherwise I can't fit you all in. You're such a big boy.'

Unfortunately for the furtive lovers, Olive *had* been missed. Emily had not been asleep and saw her companion steal from the room. After a few seconds she got up from her own bed and peeped around the door, just in time to see Olive disappear into one of the adjoining rooms. Curiosity getting the better of her, she padded towards the door. Then suddenly, hearing voices coming from the stairs, scurried back to her own room. After a few moments she checked to see if the coast was clear then ventured out again, tiptoeing back to the headmaster's door which, in Olive's haste, had been left slightly ajar. Putting her ear to the door Emily initially heard nothing, until Matron's familiar voice broke the silence. 'You have been an awfully bad boy again, Alistair, and will have to be severely punished!'

'Oh, Matron, please do; six of the best. I am fully deserving of it, for I am such a flagitious boy!'

Her heart pounding, Emily gently pushed open the door, then bit her lip hard at the sight that met her eyes. The headmaster was kneeling on the bed, naked except for his nightcap. The woman was squatting beside him, equally naked, slapping his buttocks hard with the palm of her hand.

'You… are… a… very… naughty… boy,' Matron gasped rhythmically as she administered her blows. 'A… very… very… very… wicked… boy!'

'Ohhh, I warrant such maltreatment!' cried the head. 'Harder please, Matron, aaaaghhh!'

Emily could watch no longer, feeling a warm flush between her legs that made her gulp. Muffling giggles with her hand, she scuttled back to her room, worried that she might be discovered. After about 10 minutes the door opened, and Matron stumbled back inside. The older woman gazed briefly at the girl, unnatural thoughts in her head, before belching and collapsing on her own bed. Emily's heart was still pounding inside her breast, but it was all she could do to stifle laughter, her eyes wet with strange emotions.

*

The next day was something of an anti-climax. The weather was cool and showery, and the players were on and off the field most of the day. By 4 o'clock the rain had intensified to such a degree that the umpires were sadly forced to abandon the match as a draw, with Heaton's score at 129-6.

A week later the school broke up for the summer holidays.

# 11 – KING AND COUNTRY

*How the mist swirls around old England*
*And when it lifts, reveals a savage new dawn,*
*Conceived in blood, and a million empty graves,*
*Await the sons of old England.*

JOHN BIGGLESWORTH – *The Sons of Old England*

Twelve months passed. Freddie Wright-Herbert had failed several exams, no doubt due in some part to his various extracurricular activities but was permitted to stay and re-sit them. This was only to the advantage of Weston House, who finally won the Wankeen Cup thanks to a century and six wickets from Freddie. Weakened by the loss of Smelling and Harvey-Winford, who had both gone up to Cambridge, Gentleman House failed even to make the final.

Jack Bigglesworth, Billy Hill, Will Fulton and Calvin Moseley all flourished academically in the lower sixth, as well as on the cricket field. Sadly, the enigmatic joker Thomas Banter was not among them, having left suddenly following a frightful scandal allegedly involving a goat, a cucumber and some sticking plaster. Tommy had gone before anyone at the school realised what had occurred. There was a rumour that his father had been imprisoned, thereby terminating the poor boy's continuing financial support. The school could simply not afford the embarrassment.

In fact, nobody ever really found out the truth, but poor Tommy's life was in tatters, with no hope of continuing his academic career. His stepmother disowned him and ostracised by his remaining family, he turned to drink and ended up destitute and a vagrant, his life probably saved by the outbreak of war, which allowed him to enlist.

By the following cricket season Jack and Billy were regular members of the school 1st XI, along with Jimmy Wright-Herbert. Renshaw and Dangerfield had gone up to Oxford. Freddie continued to dominate on the sports field, but having lost his most intimate associates, was more often seen studying intensely, for if he failed again, he would not get to university, meaning disgrace for his family. He need not have worried. He passed all subsequent examinations with flying colours and won a place at Trinity Hall, Cambridge. In the 1913 Wickham Dale versus Heaton match he scored another century and took 13 wickets as the Widdlers won by an innings. Freddie Wright-Herbert was now being spoken of as a future England cricketer before he had even appeared in a first-class match.

As an undergraduate in the 1914 season Freddie was immediately selected for the Cambridge team and starred in victories over Middlesex, the MCC and the University of Oxford. In early August he turned out as an amateur for Middlesex, scoring 100 against Surrey at the Oval. By this time, he had already made 1,000 first-class runs at an average of more than 50 and bagged nearly 60 wickets at the cost of 18 runs each. Were it not for the fact that England played no Test matches that summer, he would undoubtedly have been selected for an England trial. Sadly, the Surrey fixture proved to be his last match that summer. On 4 August Britain declared war on Germany and all cricket fixtures were suspended indefinitely.

*

It was the last week of the 1914 summer term at Wickham Dale. Cricket matches had come and gone, much as they had in previous years, but now an air of uncertainty hung over the senior students. The political situation in Europe was slowly deteriorating following the assassination of the Austrian Archduke Ferdinand in Sarajevo at the end of June. It seemed at first a distant event, but the situation in the Balkans had been troubling the politics of the continent for some time, with both Austria and Russia keen to expand their ailing empires, while France and Germany were renewing their ancient antagonism. The latter had lately entered an arms race with the British and both countries were busy building bigger and faster battleships; the Germans were beginning to challenge Britain as a colonial empire. The assassination of Ferdinand by Serbian extremists provoked Austria to declare war on Serbia. Russia sided with fellow Slavs, and Germany with Austria, so setting the alliances against each other as Europe sleepwalked into a major conflict.

'So, what will the Russians do now, sir?' asked Billy Hill as he strolled into the school grounds with Professor Brooman in the last days of July, shortly before the college broke up for the summer holidays.

'The Russians claim to be the protectors of their fellow Slavs, my boy, but they have their eyes on territorial gains from the sick Austro-Hungarian Empire. If the Austrians attack Serbia, the Russians will mobilise.'

'But what has that got to do with England, sir?'

It was a warm day, much as it had been all summer. A cricket match was playing out on the Short Field between two teams of juniors, and everything seemed so tranquil. Somewhere a church bell was tolling, and birds were singing as if they had not a care in the world. The professor put on his most serious academic face. 'If Russia declares war on Austria, then Germany will declare on Russia. The French have a military alliance with the Russians and will confront Germany. Britain is neutral but is unlikely to stand by and let France be attacked. Think of it as a pack of cards, going down flip-flop.'

'But it all seems so silly,' said Billy. 'I don't understand any of it. Why should England go to war over a quarrel at the other end of Europe?'

'You have a simple way of looking at things, Mister Hill, but your perception is not incorrect. It is kings, emperors and politicians that start wars, but it is the common man that must wage them.'

'But *we* are not common men, sir.'

'No, indeed we are not, but you, my boy, and those like you, the favoured elite who are so fortunate to be the recipients of the finest education in the world, are the ones that must show the way. You are young gentlemen and must set the example. If there should be a war, and it looks like there will be, it will be a conflict the like of which we have never witnessed before and will probably never see again. Britain's army is small and is recruited to police our colonies, not fight mighty pitched battles against powerful industrial nations. We will need many officers, leaders – the youthful product of our privileged classes.' Brooman paused for Billy to take in what he had said, then continued. 'You know, cricket is a wonderful metaphor for the outside world. In hours spent on a cricket field a boy will learn lessons of life that no school instruction can ever instil, the lessons of self-reliance, calmness and courage, and many other excellent qualities, which will better fit you to discharge whatever your duty may be and face any difficulties that the future may bring. The physical and moral benefits of playing the game of cricket will see you through life, whatever fate has in store.'

'I never thought of it that way,' puffed Billy, struggling to keep pace as the master strode purposefully along. 'Will I have to fight, sir? I don't think I'd make much of a warrior.'

Brooman smiled. 'We will all have to do our duty if a war comes, whatever that may be.' He considered briefly, then continued, 'You know, my grandfather fought in the Crimea. He was a cavalry officer and rode with the Light Brigade. He was gravely wounded and captured but survived to tell his tale. Then my brother was killed in the South African war at little more than your age. They are much honoured in my family.'

'I don't think I could be a hero, sir. Hey, there's Jack!'

Jack Bigglesworth came running up in excited fashion. 'Sir, sir! I just heard the news from my father. Austria has declared war on Serbia. Father says the Russians will declare war on Austria, then Germany will oppose Russia, then France will support the Russians and Germany will attack France. England won't be able to keep out of it until the peace of Europe is restored. Isn't it exciting! I shall apply to join up if required, at least when I'm 19. I'll be happy to give university a miss, at least for a while. It will be all over by Christmas anyway, won't it? What a spree it will be! What an adventure!'

Brooman smiled weakly and replied,' Yes, Mister Bigglesworth. It will be an adventure alright.'

\*

The following day the final cricket fixture of the summer took place in the Long Field against Christminster College, London, which was traditionally the last game of the season. There was a strange air of excitement hovering over the proceedings, perhaps mixed with one of foreboding. Professor Brooman sat and watched the boys at their game, just as he had done hundreds of times before, but on this occasion, he was not contented, knowing that when the school broke up he would not see many of them again. They were so full of life – the immortality of youth. To them, their very existence was an adventure and many yearned for the enterprise of a just war and the glory it may bring, regardless of the consequences, but the master knew that beyond any glory may lie misery and suffering, and for some boys a death before they had barely lived.

He watched the careful, resilient Bigglesworth and wondered what kind of a soldier he might make. Billy Hill, the tubby boy, butt of much chaffing, yet he sensed there a latent aptitude and adaptability; Will Fulton, the handsome lad who perhaps knew more than was good for him; Calvin Moseley, the belligerent boy, always spoiling for a fight and agitating for things that should not have been concerning him; his younger brother Roland, so strong and athletic with the face of an angel – he was too young to fight, at least for a few years.

He watched them all at their game, batting, bowling, fielding, full of the joys of competition. He sat and watched them for a while, his eyes moist, then could watch no more. He walked slowly away, dwelling on a generation about to be lost forever. The professor was no longer present as the evening shadows began to fall across the field and the nearby church bell commenced its dreary rhythm.

Billy Hill bowled to the last Christminster batsman, who edged to Jack Bigglesworth in the slips and the match was over. The boys shook hands and bounced gaily off the field, chattering happily away, for the last time.

The last ball of summer.

Henceforth there would be a bigger field to play on and a less sporting game to play.

*

On the outbreak of war, the Wickham Dale 1st XI volunteered to a man, answering the call of the secretary of state for war Lord Kitchener's plea for a million men. By the end of 1914 over one million civilians had indeed rallied to the colours, though it would be some time before they could all be trained and fit enough to be sent to France. In the meantime, Britain's small standing army had to bear the brunt. The British Expeditionary Force (BEF), just a few divisions strong, found itself facing the full might of the German Army as it swept through Belgium. The force stood its ground at Mons and Le Cateau but was forced to retreat to keep line with the retiring French Army on its right. Eventually a gap appeared between the advancing German First and Second Armies, strategically exploited by the Allies to throw the invaders back from the gates of Paris.

The Germans dug in, the British and French likewise. By the close of 1914 the Western Front had ground to a stalemate, with a line of trenches stretching from the North Sea to the Swiss border separating the combatants. It would not be over by Christmas.

Attempts by the French and British to break the deadlock in 1915 proved fruitless, the killing grounds only becoming larger. By now the 'Old Contemptibles'* of the original BEF were no more, replaced by Territorial Units. Kitchener's new citizen army would not see action until 1916 and many of the new soldiers had formed into 'pals'' battalions from a similar area or background and class, assembling to live and fight alongside each other just as they may have worked and played together in peacetime. One such battalion was the 10th (Sportsmen's) Royal London, a group of soldiers from a sporting background of whom many were professional cricketers and footballers. Amateurs such as the boys from Wickham Dale and other public schools were also in its ranks. Their time would soon come.

*The BEF was reputedly described as a 'contemptible little army' by the German Kaiser Wilhelm II, though the phrase was later believed to have meant a 'contemptibly little army', referring to its size and not its calibre.

# 12 – THE CLOSE OF THE GOLDEN AGE

*Those giants of the Golden Age*
*Hold forth upon the cricket's page,*
*Forever remembered.*

JOHN BIGGLESWORTH – *The Giants of the Golden Age*

The year 1914 saw the end of cricket's so called 'Golden Age', a period that gained more acclaim in retrospect than it probably deserved. Cricket was a sport that was still to a large degree dominated by 'amateurs', gentlemen cricketers who had been educated at private schools and university. The professionals provided the backbone of English county sides in the early years of the 20th century, but the two classes often had different dressing rooms and gates, through which they reached the field.

Test cricket was still in its infancy, with only England, Australia and South Africa having played any first-class international fixtures. In 1912, the first year of our story, all three countries took part in a triangular Test series in England, though the experiment was mostly ruined by bad weather. England emerged the winners, defeating Australia in the ninth and final game of the series after both countries had beaten South Africa convincingly.

There were no home Tests in the English summer of 1913, but the following winter England toured South Africa, a series in which Freddie Wright-Herbert might have played had he gone up to Cambridge a year earlier. The tourists easily won the first Test in Durban by an innings and 157 runs. The South African captain, H.W. Taylor, made 109 of his side's total of 182 in their first innings, England's Sidney Barnes taking five wickets for 57 runs. The visitors' reply of 450 included 119 from their skipper J.W.H.T. Douglas and 82 from Jack Hobbs, with the Honourable L.H. (later 3rd Baron) Tennyson (grandson of the poet) contributing 52 on his debut. Barnes bagged another five wickets in South Africa's second innings, thereby becoming the first bowler to take 150 Test match wickets in only his 24th international match.

England were equally dominant in the Second Test in Johannesburg in which Barnes took 17 wickets for 157, a record that stood until Jim Laker's 19 for 90 against Australia at Manchester's Old Trafford ground in 1956. Wilfred Rhodes made 152 in England's only innings of 403, becoming the first international player to reach the 'double' of 1,000 runs and 100 wickets. C.P. Mead added 102 and A.E. Relf 63, while South Africa were dismissed for 160 and 231, going down by an innings and 12 runs.

The next Test, also played in Johannesburg after a break of just one day, was more of a contest. Hobbs top-scored with 92 in England's first innings of 238. Jack Hearne bagged 5-49 when the home side were bowled out for 151, after which Mead (86) and Douglas (77) helped to increase England's lead to 395. The South Africans were in with a shout when Taylor (70) and Zulch (82) put up 153 for their first wicket until Barnes induced a collapse, six wickets going down for just 20. Although Blankenburg boldly hit 59 going in at number nine, the total fell short by 91 runs, Barnes claiming another eight wickets to make it 35 victims in England's three victories to date.

Sidney Barnes, the greatest bowler of his generation – some would argue the greatest of all time – was reputedly a prickly character who spent most of his career outside county cricket. He was nearly 41 at the time of this series and worked as a clerk in a Staffordshire colliery. At the outbreak of war, he was too old to enlist and plied his trade until 1925 with Saltaire in the Bradford League, where he took an amazing 904 wickets at an average of only 5.26, including 100 in a season on five occasions.

Barnes took a further 14 wickets in the Fourth Test in Durban, but this time the tourists had to hang on for a draw at 154-5 having been set 313 to win. This was to be his last match for England as he declined to play in the final Test due to a dispute with the management, but his total of 49 wickets at an average of 10.93 has never been bettered. In seven matches against the South Africans, he claimed 83 wickets at 9.85 and the remainder of his 189 in 20 Tests against Australia. He had 10 wickets in a match six times and five or more in an innings on 12 occasions.

Even without him England won the Fifth Test easily by 10 wickets and the series by 4-0. It would be six years and 289 days – the longest ever interval – before another Test match was played, at the Sydney Cricket Ground in December 1920. Incredibly, six England players – Hobbs, Hearne, Rhodes, Douglas, Woolley and wicket-keeper Strudwick – straddled the two matches.

There were also no home Tests in the English summer of 1914, though experts believed Freddie Wright-Herbert would undoubtedly have been selected had there been international fixtures. The season was abandoned in early August at the outbreak of hostilities. Surrey was confirmed as county champions, having won 15 of their 26 matches to that point. Middlesex finished second and Kent (the 1913 champions) third. Yorkshire were fourth, with W.G. Grace's old county Gloucestershire last, after winning just one of their 22 matches. At 47, Jack Hearne finished top of the batting averages with 1828 runs at an average of 76.16. Surrey's Jack Hobbs was the leading run-scorer with 2,499 (average 62.47). Colin Blythe of Kent was the leading wicket-taker with 159 at 15.03 each. He was to become one of the war victims, dying at Passchendaele in November 1917.

The leading all-rounder was the England captain J.W.H.T. Douglas, popularly known as 'Johnny Won't Hit Today', a combination of his dour batting and initials, who scored 1,151 runs (39.68) and took 118 wickets (18.80). Freddie's performances in the truncated season earned him a respectable seventh in the national batting averages and ninth place in the bowling list. But now duty called, and he had a bigger match to play.

The ensuing war claimed several famed cricketers. The previously mentioned Colin Blythe had retired by the time it broke out, having taken 2,506 wickets, including 100 in 19 Tests. Blythe was a sensitive soul and an excellent musician but suffered from epilepsy and other nervous complaints. He joined the Kent Fortress Engineers and was killed working on a railway, aged 38. A memorial stands at the entrance to the Spitfire cricket ground in Canterbury. His two shrapnel-ridden wallets, removed from his dead body, are displayed in the county museum there.

The Australian fast bowler Albert Cotter was killed at Beersheba in the Middle East campaign at the age of 33. The promising Warwickshire bowler Percy Jeeves (who gave his name to P.G. Wodehouse's famous character) died in 1916 while serving with the Royal Warwickshire regiment. The famous Clifton College boy Arthur Edward Jeune Collins, who scored 628 not out and took 11 wickets in a house match back in 1899 when only 14 years old, also fell in the fray. He joined the Royal Engineers after leaving school and played little serious cricket thereafter. He was killed at the first battle of Ypres in November 1914.

The most mourned death of them all, in cricketing terms, was that of the 'Grand Old Man' of English cricket, W.G. Grace, giant of the Victorian era and arguably the most celebrated player of all time, who passed away in 1915 at the age of 67. A golden age of cricket had finally come to an end, never to return.

The English team suffered more from the war than did Australia and South Africa. In the 1920–21 Ashes Series in Australia the tourists were thrashed 5-0 before Australia stretched their winning run against the old enemy to eight convincing victories in the summer of 1921. England stopped the rot with draws in the last two Tests, the Hon. Lionel Tennyson having taken over the captaincy from Douglas.

They were giants, wonderful giants of old.

# SPORTSMEN!

## JOIN TOGETHER TRAIN TOGETHER

## EMBARK TOGETHER FIGHT TOGETHER!

## ENLIST IN THE

## SPORTSMEN'S 1000

### SPORTS

### THE MEDAL OF MEDALS

#### INFORMATION:

#### SPORTSMEN'S 1000

#### PHONE DEFENCE 75

Or call between 1 and 6 pm on weekdays.
Automobile club/Equitable Building 101 Swanson Street

## PLAY UP, PLAY UP AND PLAY THE GAME

# 13 – THROUGH THE DARK CLOUD SHINING

*O why, O why, am I so shy?*
*Why did I let the years go by?*
*You would lead me 'ere I go*
*Though my love I'd never show*

JOHN BIGGLESWORTH – *To Cathy on her 19th birthday*

During the autumn of 1915 Lieutenant Jack Bigglesworth returned home from the Western Front for a few days' leave. His parents lived in a comfortable pile just north of Brighton on the Sussex Downs. He was an only child; his mother and father had married late in life. His father was a retired businessman, now in his early 70s and not in the best of health. He welcomed his only son into the drawing room.

'How are you, Father?' asked Jack.

The old fellow offered a lame hand and said nothing until he had sat down, stiffly. 'Help yourself to a drink, my boy,' he commanded gruffly. 'Or are you still abstemious?'

'Thank you. I've developed a taste for whisky recently. It helps steady the nerves when the Boche are shelling us.'

'Well done, my son. The army will make a man of you yet.' The old man looked drawn, his face pale and his once-thick hair now white and stringy. Jack had never been close to his father. He had been abroad working through much of his son's childhood and they saw little of each other. Jack was always given the impression that he was something of a disappointment to his parents.

'Fighting in a war does not make one a man then?' Jack sounded irritated.

The old man waved his hand in a dismissive gesture. 'Don't be obstreperous now, my lad. You're sounding just like your mother!'

'Where is Mother?'

'She'll be along shortly. Probably fussing over something and nothing as usual. Now, tell me about the war. How are things going? Will it be over soon?'

Jack sipped his drink and pondered for a while before answering. 'No, Father, it won't be over soon. Our boys are being sacrificed in their thousands by pointless attacks. The generals have no conception; they just throw men at the enemy, flesh and blood against iron and steel. There is no coherent strategy. The men are in good heart, but they are lions led by asses. We do not have enough heavy guns. If we did, we would not have enough shells to fire. There is no glory in this war. All that jingoistic nonsense they give us about sacrifice for the greater good, and king and country, was just poppycock! There is only misery, suffering and death in war.'

His father coughed. 'Don't like to hear that kind of talk. We're all in this together.'

'We? Just who exactly are 'We'? People back here have no conception of what is really happening out there. The politicians...'

'Do you still play cricket?'

Jack was somewhat thrown by the sudden change of subject. 'No, don't get much time these days. There's a war on if you hadn't noticed.'

'Pity, you were quite promising at one time.'

'Johnny, darling!' Jack's intended terse reply was cut off by his mother's entry into the room. She was a small, grey woman but full of sparkle and gaiety. 'Oh, you look so dashing in your uniform and that moustache really suits you.' She perched on her toes to kiss her son's cheek. 'Guess what, Johnny? The Ketteridges are coming to dinner. Kitty is so looking forward to seeing you. Hilda says she talks of nothing else.' The family were next-door neighbours, if a house half a mile away could be called neighbourly. Kitty was their daughter and one year younger than Jack. The pair had been inseparable childhood friends in another world. Kitty's mother, Hilda, was the best friend of Jack's mother, Rose.

It proved to be an uncomfortable evening. Rose twittered away in her fashion, attempting to create a convivial atmosphere as the Ketteridges pestered Jack with questions about the war in France, which he fielded politely and diplomatically, if perhaps not necessarily truthfully, avoiding any offence. During brief silences and mouthfuls of food he raised his head to observe Kitty staring at him, though she averted her gaze when she saw him looking. He had not seen her for many years and in that time, she had grown into a handsome young woman, if perhaps not overly beautiful. She was slim and bubbly but had a sad smile, and a bob of short, black hair around her soft, oval face.

After the meal Jack excused himself, poured a whisky and soda and wandered into the garden. The evening air was cool, and he closed his eyes, trying not to think of France. Suddenly he felt a butterfly touch on his arm.

'Hello, Johnny, I've been dying to talk to you. Can we walk for a bit?' Kitty held on to Jack's arm gently as they slowly padded down the long garden. It was flanked by fruit trees and huge rose bushes.

'Only my mother ever calls me Johnny.'

'Then I shall be mother,' she laughed.

For a while they did not speak. He felt the softness and fragrance of her body. It was so close it disturbed him, though he could not reason why. As a child he had often felt uncomfortable in her presence, though he always had a fondness for her. Eventually he broke the silence. 'I met up with many of my school friends. They are in the same battalion. It's called the Sportsmen's Battalion. Sometimes I wish...'

'What, Johnny?'

'I wish... I wish I were back there. At school I mean. I was happy there.'

'But you're not, are you. You are a soldier now, doing your duty. You do look splendid in your uniform. I'm so proud of you. Tell me about France. Is it really as awful as everyone says?'

Jack looked at her but instead of returning his gaze she stared ahead into the oncoming night. 'It's not so bad really,' he lied, 'if you ignore the stench and the rats and lice in the trenches and keep your head down when the shells are flying over.'

'But you are not at the front all the time?'

'No, when we are out of the line, I have a nice little billet with an estaminet nearby.'

'Do you have a woman out there?'

It seemed an odd question for her to ask so he did not reply but looked again at her soft face in the moonlight. The little girl with the waist-length hair and toothy grin was long gone, but he could still see the child in her.

'Do you get on with your men?'

'I think they may chaff me a bit when my back is turned but they're not a bad lot really.'

'If I catch them chaffing you, I shall jolly well give them a piece of my mind!' she giggled, squeezing his sleeve.

It seemed a silly thing to say but Jack hardly cared. Managing a weak smile, he added, 'I wasn't cut out to be a leader, Kitty.'

'Of course, you were! You are my hero and I never stop thinking of you. I worry about you so much. Oh, Johnny, I've hardly seen you these past years.' She rested her head on his shoulder as they walked along together arm in arm. Jack captured her sweet fragrance again, which made him catch his breath. 'I really do think of you constantly,' she said.

'Really? I had no idea. Mother never mentioned you in her letters.' He felt a strange tingle through his body. She had always just been a childhood friend. He had never thought of her in any other way. Then again, he had always felt dead inside, never having any real feelings for anyone.

She stopped and faced him, taking both his hands and trying to look profoundly serious. 'Well then, that's very remiss of her. I know she's never really liked me.' Kitty looked down to her feet, then asked again, 'Do you have a woman over there, Johnny?'

'No, some of the chaps go to, you know, one of those places, but not me.'

'Then, could I be your sweetheart, Johnny? All the girls at school have sweethearts at the front and write to each other. Sometimes they laugh at me and call me a plain Jane because I wear glasses and am always reading and studying. Oh, please say yes!'

Jack felt slightly overwhelmed, never having thought of her that way. He suddenly felt an urge to pull her into his arms and kiss her, but something stopped him. It would be like kissing his sister, so he replied, 'But that's awful! How can they be so unkind?'

'They're not really.' She let go of his hands and they continued walking, arm in arm. 'They are good friends but sometimes they tease me. Will you write to me, Johnny? I can write to you. Do you still write those poems? Send me a poem from France.'

So many questions. 'Yes, I'd like that,' said Jack after another pause, 'but they censor our letters so as not to give vital information away to the enemy.'

'But that's awful! How can other people read your personal correspondence?'

'That's the way of it, Kitty. One day everyone will know the truth about this war, but now no one wants to listen.'

'Then one day you must make them listen, and if you don't then I will.' Jack smiled at her. As a girl she had always been tenacious.

After another pregnant pause he asked, 'Will you go to university?'

'Mummy and Daddy want me go next month. They've found a place for me, but I would rather do something patriotic instead, like becoming a nurse or a bus conductress.'

Jack laughed. 'And waste your fine education? I can't see you on the buses somehow.'

'It's not funny. Things are changing, Johnny my darling. England is never going to be the same again once this awful war is over. We women are doing all sorts of jobs while the men are away fighting – working in munition factories, on the trams and in the Land Army, driving tractors and mucking out on farms. When this war is over, we shall have the vote.'

'Good God, don't tell me you're a suffragette!'

'I am a little bit of one,' she chuckled, 'but I have to keep it quiet because Mummy and Daddy don't approve of such things.'

'You should follow your conscience. Women must have the same rights as men. It's only fair.'

'I'm glad you agree with me, Johnny. If you didn't then I'd be jolly cross with you!' She turned and glared at him, putting on her determined face again. 'What's the point of a good education if they just marry me off to some chinless toff so I can have his babies and organise his dinner parties.'

Jack laughed again. 'You were always a sparky little thing.'

Her face softened. 'I'm not so little anymore, Johnny. I'm a woman now.'

That much was obvious to Jack. As children they had been like brother and sister, but children grow up and their feelings for each other had changed. He had no idea she felt this way. He was always a solitary person, even more so now. Something ached inside him, an emptiness he could not put into words. They walked awhile, then he felt her shiver. 'We'd better go back inside, I'm getting cold.' They turned back towards the house, and she squeezed his arm once more. 'The war will be over soon, won't it, Johnny? We will prevail, won't we?'

'Nobody wins a war, Kitty. Men fight and men die, but nobody wins.'

As they walked back inside Jack could not fail to notice a disapproving look on the faces of Hilda and his mother. 'Oh, there you are,' said Hilda snootily.

There was no such sentimentality for Freddie Wright-Herbert: when war broke out his family used their influence to get him a commission in The Grenadier Guards, but he found life there a mite too rich for his tastes so transferred to the 10th (Sportsmen's) Royal London regiment in early 1915. While at the Officers' Training Camp at Bexhill in Sussex he got into a spot of bother cutting a swathe through the local female population. After getting drunk one night and availing himself of the services of the local brothel, he defiantly refused to pay anything for his pleasure, telling the girl in question that it was 'her patriotic duty to open her legs for king and country'. After a bit of a kerfuffle with the Military Police Freddie compromised by rewarding the woman with a symbolic shilling.

The war dragged on into 1916, when the politicians were more determined to affect a breakthrough, following the failure of Winston Churchill's disastrous campaign to attack Turkey (now an ally of the Central Powers Germany and Austria) through the Dardanelles. Kitchener's citizen army was now coming online, reinforcing the Western front.

Early in that year the Germans were determined to knock the French out of the war and thus concentrated all their forces on attacking the ancient fortress city of Verdun in Eastern France, close to the Franco-German border. To relieve the pressure, the French High Command pleaded with the British to take the offensive further north. The place eventually chosen for this assault was the region of Picardy in the valley of the River Somme, previously a quiet sector in the line of entrenchments. Here, Britain's volunteer army was poised to see action for the first time, including many of the boys from Wickham Dale, most of whom were now junior officers in various regiments.

Their day of reckoning was coming.

# 14 – KITTY AND EMILY TAKE THE OFFENSIVE

*When the boys play the girls at cricket*
*Be sure there is grass upon the wicket!*

FREDDIE WRIGHT-HERBERT – *Uncovered Wickets*

A few weeks before the 'big push' was due to take place, Lieutenant Jack Bigglesworth of the 7th Battalion, Middlesex Regiment was granted a short spell of leave. Rather than visit home, he arranged to stay at the Piccadilly Park Hotel in London, where he met Kitty Ketteridge for dinner. As agreed, they had been corresponding for some time.

Tranquilised by several whisky and sodas, Jack spoke little during the meal, while Kitty twittered away in the fashion of her mother. She clearly had made a great effort to impress, looking so different now from how Jack remembered her – dressed in a low-cut, frilly outfit with a head band and feather adorning her bob of black hair and prompting many heads to turn. Gone was the rough and tumble tomboy of their childhood days, which had been replaced by a confident, fully grown woman. Her big, sad brown eyes and pale skin were softer than he recalled.

He had never been comfortable in the company of women and consequently felt more uneasy in her presence than usual. 'You've filled out a bit,' he observed neutrally.

'Yes, Johnny, I've been working so hard for the Women's Land Army, building up my muscles,' she grinned, pouring herself another glass of champagne. 'We've been slaving away on this big farm in Buckinghamshire.'

'You look well on it. You have certainly grown up. What happened to working on the buses?'

Kitty frowned. 'Of course I have, you old silly. I am grown up. You look thin, my sweet.'

'My nerves are bad. There's a big attack coming, but please don't say anything.'

'You mean there may be German spies listening,' she tittered.

'Don't joke about it, Kitty, they are everywhere. I think some of the waiters look a bit suspicious. This is the biggest offensive ever undertaken. If we break through, the war could be over in weeks. I must lead my men over the top. It terrifies me.'

He took another gulp of whisky.

'Oh Johnny, I couldn't bear it if you were killed. Please be careful!'

'I'm an officer, Kitty, I must lead by example, from the front.'

'You know Julian was killed,' she said sombrely.

'Yes, I'm so sorry. Your parents must be devasted.'

'He was my brother, but I never cared for him that much. He was horrid and used to bully you, as I recall.'

'Yes,' Jack agreed, 'I never liked him, but I'm sorry he's dead.'

An uneasy silence followed as Jack searched for some words to break the lull in their conversation. Kitty took another mouthful of cheap champagne, too much, and burped embarrassingly. 'Steady, old girl,' he warned. 'Go easy on the champers. You're not used to it.'

'I don't care!' she replied, so loudly that an elderly couple on the next table began to look at her disapprovingly. 'I'm a big girl and can drink as much as I like, and now I'm going to have one of your cigarettes.' She opened Jack's silver cigarette case and took one out, clumsily lighting it with the candle on the table.

'Kitty!' cried Jack, looking in surprise at her, 'when did you start smoking?' He looked about nervously. Women smoking was frowned upon in such establishments.

'Just now,' she coughed. 'When did you? I thought you hated it.'

Jack fingered the shiny case. 'It helps my nerves, along with the whisky. A fellow officer gave it to me just before he went out on night patrol. He said to keep it if...'

'If he didn't come back?'

'Yes.'

'Oh darling, I'm so sorry. Were you close?'

'Not really. It's best not to make too many friends at the front.' She puffed away pettishly, causing Jack to remark, 'That's not the first cigarette you've had?'

'No, some of the girls on the farm smoke and I steal a puff sometimes.'

Jack ran out of conversation again. Thankfully, Kitty stubbed out her cigarette then looked at him earnestly, reaching across the table and taking his hands in hers. 'Johnny, I've a terrible confession to make,' she announced.

'Oh dear, nothing serious I hope.' Jack was feeling drunk, desperately trying to keep his composure.

'I told mother I was going up to London to stay with an old school friend tonight.'

Jack glanced at his watch. 'Yes, it's getting late. You should be going.'

'Oh, you are an old silly, missing the point as always!'

'Sorry, Kitty, I...'

'Remember when we were little, and pretended to get married? You made a posy of flowers for me from the garden, and we ran away into the woods for our honeymoon.'

Jack grimaced, not liking where the conversation might be leading. 'Yes, we got lost and your father's gamekeeper had to come and find us. My father gave me a frightful thrashing. I couldn't sit down for a week!'

'Poor darling, I was always getting you into trouble. They wouldn't let us play together for ages afterwards. I sulked the whole time and wouldn't eat.'

Jack smiled at the memory. What made you bring this up now?'

'I lied to mother,' Kitty confessed. 'There is no school friend.'

'Sorry, I... I don't understand.'

'Oh, Johnny, you are such a dimwit sometimes! You have a room here, don't you?

'Yes, but...'

'Then can't we pretend we're married again?'

119

Jack was flabbergasted, his heart jumping. 'Kitty, what are you suggesting? Are you out of your mind? You can't be serious! You don't know what you're saying!'

She looked deeply into his hazel eyes. 'I know exactly what I'm saying. Oh, Johnny, I want to stay with you tonight. We may never see each other again!'

The light finally dawned on Jack. Unable to believe what she was proposing, he suddenly felt a tingle in his loins and butterflies in his stomach, just like when he had walked out to face Pongo Smelling in the Wankeen Cup cricket final. The elderly couple on the next table had cottoned on to their conversation, the woman scowling most disapprovingly.

'But Kitty, it's not right, and anyway...'

Kitty gave him a withering look. 'Am I so repulsive then, that you can't make love to me!'

'No, it's not that, you're...'

'I'm what?' She looked at him angrily, but Jack knew the routine. She would pretend to be annoyed and upset with him, then soften and go all girly, and he would be her slave.

'No, you're... lovely. It's... it's... just that, well, they are really stuffy here. They might not let us...'

'I know, I've thought of that,' she brightened, rummaging in her purse and bringing out a ring which she put on her wedding finger. 'It's my grandmother's old ring which she left me. Look, now I'm Mrs Bigglesworth,' she gushed, waving her hand about, attracting more disdainful looks from the couple on the adjoining table.

Jack flushed with embarrassment. 'Kitty, please, keep your voice down, you're attracting attention!' He thought he heard the woman saying, 'shameless hussy'.

'Don't care!'

He squirmed in his chair, suddenly feeling a great urge to visit the lavatory. 'Look, darling,' she whispered softly, 'it's quite safe. We women know about these things. You do trust me, don't you? Don't you want to know what it's like? We may never have another chance to be together.'

It was true. He had never known a woman, at least not in the biblical sense. She was right, they might not ever see each other again. He no longer cared any more what happened to himself, but he did care what happened to her. It was no use; she always got her way with him. 'Alright then,' Jack said, surrendering reluctantly, 'if you are sure.' He could hardly believe what he was saying, his heart pounding.

She smiled sweetly, as she often did when she got her way, soothing his beating breast. 'I told you, we women know about such things.'

Jack braced himself with another gulp of whisky, signed the chit for the dinner bill and got up, his knees trembling. They walked to the front desk together a trifle unsteadily, with Kitty holding on tightly to his arm. 'Room 507 please,' he said slightly nervously to the desk clerk, a smarmy-looking young man with slicked-back hair. 'My wife will be joining me tonight. We've only just got married.'

'Really, sir?' said the clerk snootily, handing over the key. Kitty made an embarrassing show of waving her ring in front of him. 'How nice for you both. Will there be anything else?'

'No thank you,' replied Jack bravely. 'Good night.'

'Good night,' giggled Kitty.

'Good night, sir, madam,' said the clerk drearily, with the air of a man who had seen it all before.

'Do you think he rumbled us?' sniggered Kitty, almost falling over as they walked to the elevator.

'Oh no,' Jack lied, 'we're quite safe.' Safe or not, he was going 'over the top' this time. He had drunk too much, and the whisky was not mixing well with the rich food he was unused to, but he no longer cared.

'You will be gentle with me, won't you, Johnny my darling?' Kitty pleaded as they tumbled into the lift.

*

Meanwhile, sitting in the same huge dining room, were Second Lieutenant William Fulton and Emily Dickens, nursing assistant at Wickham Dale College. It was not surprising that the fellow officers had not spotted each other, since at least half of the male diners were in uniform. They too had become close friends and had been corresponding since Will left for France.

'Isn't that Jack Biggleswade over there?' asked Emily, as Will ordered his food.

'What's that, my little sugar plum?'

'Over there,' she pointed.

'Bigglesworth,' corrected Will. 'He's in my brigade now. Don't recognise the floozy he's with. I didn't know the old dog had it in him! Shall we go and say hello?'

'No,' she replied forcefully. 'I need to speak to you.'

'OK, old thing, fire away.'

Emily, too, had filled out into a fine-looking young woman. She was now 20 and had freckled skin to match her fiery red hair, and a body that was curving in all the right places, though she retained the innocent look that had captivated Will from the first moment he saw her. 'It's about Matron,' she began.

'Really, how is the old dragon?'

'I can't begin to tell you,' Emily whispered, leaning across the table. 'Did you know that her and the headmaster have been at it like knives for years. It's disgusting!'

'Oh, we all knew about that,' Will said nonchalantly, 'She's a proper old bicycle. Even Freddie's been poking about in her undercarriage.'

'You never told me you knew any of this! You might have warned me.'

'Didn't want to worry you.' Will struck a match and lit his pipe. 'Not the sort of stuff one talks to a popsy about.'

'I'm not one of your popsies!' Emily said angrily.

'No, of course not. Beg pardon.'

'Anyway, I knew about Freddie. Caught them at it. Disgusting it was too, that old bag dropping her draws for a boy like that.'

'Yes, damn bad show,' agreed Will, trying not to laugh.

'But that's not the worst thing. The old bat is getting odder by the day. She's half seas over most of the time, even when on duty. The smell is awful.'

'Oh dear.'

'Yes, but even worse than that. Do you know what she said to me?'

'Do tell.'

'She said, ''You like to watch, don't you? I bet you like to excite yourself''.'

'And do you?'

'Do I what?'

'Like to watch?'

Emily looked disconcerted, as if her companion had struck a raw nerve. 'Of course I don't! What kind of a person do you think I am?' Will coughed nervously and became silent.

'Anyways,' continued Emily, recovering herself and leaning ever closer across the table, 'the absolute worst thing of all is that she is becoming awfully familiar with me, saying what a lovely girl I am, touching me and asking if I'd like to go away with her for a weekend. I tell you, Wills, she's like a perverted old witch on heat. I'm scared stiff of her. I had to tell her I was visiting my sick grandmother today. She wouldn't have given me the time off if she'd known I was meeting you. I don't think she believed me. She always warned me about you. I'm taking my nursing certificate soon and hope to leave at the end of the summer. The trouble is, I have to keep in with her because I need a good reference.'

'Goodness, it all does sound a bit ticklish,' observed Will. 'She tried it on with me once, but I threatened to report her.'

'You should have told me!'

'Perhaps I should, but while we're on the subject, how about a spot of fun tonight to cheer us both up? I'm away to France tomorrow and the little fellow could do with a bit of exercise to see me off in a good mood.'

'Willow!' she exclaimed, loud enough to attract attention. 'I hope you are not suggesting what I think you are. What kind of a girl do you think I am!'

'No, of course not, sorry old girl, only joking.'

'You weren't joking,' she sniffed, pulling a handkerchief from her pocket. 'You boys think of nothing else. Maybe Matron was right. I'm a decent girl.'

'Yes, of course you are,' said Will, backtracking. 'Don't turn on the waterworks, there's a brick.'

'You can jolly well wait until we are married. That's how it must be.'

'Ems, I really do care for you, please don't cry.'

'Well then,' she sniffed, 'that's not a genuinely nice way to show it. She dabbed her nose with her hankie. 'I was hoping you'd be sympathetic. I have to go back and face that dreadful old harridan and all you can do is think of your little chap.'

'Er... married?' queried Will, the penny dropping. 'I don't recall...'

'We can wait until the war's over if you like,' she smiled bravely.

Lieutenant Will Fulton started to fidget around in his chair, wishing he were back in the trenches.

*

Meanwhile, Freddie Wright-Herbert had also been on furlough. After a brief but necessary visit to his family seat, he travelled to Wickhamstead to renew his acquaintance with the ever-willing Polly Plunkett, spending two nights with her in the Cock and Bull Inn, which was pretty much his disposition for most of the time, then passing away the evening by drinking himself senseless. His behaviour did not go unnoticed by Polly's landlord—father Reuben, who observed to a small group of his patrons, 'That boy is not long for this world.'

# 15 – RARER GIFTS THAN GOLD

*Batsmen, bowlers, come sing and dance,*
*And play our games upon the fields of France.*

JOHN BIGGLESWORTH – *Upon the Fields of France*

The night before the big attack passed slowly. For seven days and seven nights the British heavy artillery had pounded the German positions in preparation for the assault. In his dugout beneath the reserve trench lines, Captain Freddie Wright-Herbert of the 10th Battalion, Royal London Regiment sat drinking and reminiscing with his old school chums Daniel Dangerfield and Sebastian Renshaw. It was only the second time they had been reunited since they had left Wickham Dale. Renshaw had procured a bottle of best French brandy which was shared around. They spoke of old times, school days, happier days.

'Not a bad little billet here, what?' observed Captain Dangerfield on the 7th Battalion, Middlesex Regiment. 'Better than the accommodation for us Middlesex boys down the road.'

'I only stay in the best places,' mused Freddie, nonchalantly lighting his pipe. In the distance could still be heard the British guns pounding the German positions.

Captain Renshaw, also of the 7th Battalion, Middlesex Regiment, gulped down another tot of brandy and wiped his mouth. 'Any more grog, chaps? Bottle's nearly empty.'

Corporal Tommy Banter, 10th Royal London, was busy at the back of the dugout, near Freddie's bunk. 'I say, Banter old bean, fetch that bottle of brandy from my kit, there's a good fellow,' ordered Freddie.

'I thought you were saving it for a special occasion, sir,' replied the batman.

'I was,' his officer frowned, 'but we may as well drink it now. Who knows what may happen tomorrow? Pour yourself a noggin, Banter.'

'Thank you very much, sir.'

'Actually, old boy, when you've finished what you are doing, see if you can rustle up some coffee from somewhere.' Tommy fiddled around for a bit, then scuttled up the wooden stairs and out into the open trench, relieved to be free of the frowsty atmosphere for a while. The incessant crump of the guns was louder there. He noted what a fine summer's night it was.

'Why do you keep that snivelling oik around?' asked Renshaw once Tommy was out of sight, sounding the worse for drink by this point.

'He amuses me,' said Freddie wistfully, 'and he's pretty loyal and resourceful.'

'Rum bugger if you ask me,' Danny pointed out, 'All that funny business with the goat.'

Freddie sucked deeply on his pipe and sighed. 'Case of mistaken identity, he claims.'

'What, you mean the wrong goat, ho, ho, ho!' roared Renshaw.

'Very amusing, Sebastian. I see you haven't lost your sense of humour.'

'Seen any other Widdlers about?' asked Dangerfield.

'My brother Jimmy is on trench duty tonight,' Freddie said. 'Young Fulton's about somewhere.'

'That Bigglesworth boy is in my company,' stated Danny.

'He's a rum bugger too,' said Sebastian. 'Stuck up his own bum, so I heard.'

'Steady enough sort of chap,' said his commanding officer. 'Keeps himself to himself. Bit of a loner, what? Wasn't interested when the officers toddled off to Arras for some physical relaxation, as I recall.'

'I say, you don't think he's a bottom-pumper, do you?' laughed Renshaw.

'I don't think so. Spends most of his time writing reams of poetry to some bit of fluff back in Blighty.'

No one spoke for a few moments. Freddie seemed preoccupied, drawing heavily on his pipe. Renshaw emptied another measure of brandy into his cracked cup. 'Don't know about you, but all this grog's making me deuced randy. Freddie, I don't suppose...?'

'No!' said Freddie firmly.

'What about your man Banter? Think he'd be up for a brisk buggering?'

'Sebastian,' Dangerfield intervened, 'if you're so desperate why not hop along to the latrines and pop one off there?'

'What, in all that shit! Not bally likely! Must say though, can't get a line on these French tarts. Too damn scrawny if you want to know. Not much to look at either.'

'Surely you only come calling at the tradesman's entrance, Sebastian,' offered Freddie drily.

'Ho, ho, ho, ho! not wrong there, old boy! A bumhole's a bumhole, regardless of what's on the other end of it.'

'That's an interesting philosophy, Sebastian,' observed Dangerfield. 'I must remember that when I rejoin polite society.'

'It might all be academic in the morning,' opined Freddie, a distant look in his eyes.

'What do you mean by that?' asked Sebastian, 'Brigade reckon it'll be a walk in the park. Some of the chaps in my company play for Middlesex Wanderers association football team and they plan to kick a few balls across no man's land.'

Danny Dangerfield, despite his occasional facetious manner, had matured into an accomplished soldier. He was well respected by his senior officers and his men, unlike Renshaw, whose continual bluster was not popular. 'Sebastian,' he mused, 'the attack will fail.'

'Don't be a dunderhead! Nothing could have lived through our barrage!'

'Danny's right,' confirmed Freddie, returning to the land of the living. 'We pushed up a forward trench to within a couple of hundred yards of the German fortifications. Will Fulton went for a recce yesterday. Much of their wire is still intact. Worse still he spotted dozens of unexploded shells sticking out of the ground. Did you know our artillery have been firing shrapnel shells because there's not enough big stuff to bowl over? Shrapnel is useless against anything but flesh and bone. Once our barrage stops the Huns will come scurrying out of their underground shelters like rats out of a hole, spoiling for a fight. Most of them are in the rear trenches anyway.'

Renshaw said nothing, taking another mouthful of brandy. 'You boys are lucky,' said Danny to Freddie. 'The 10th is opening the batting tomorrow because they are an untried unit and have a better chance of getting over there before Fritz brings on his quickies. It's the later waves that will cop all the bouncers, once they've got the range and figured out the tactics.'

'All twaddle and balderdash!' blustered Sebastian. 'The Middlesex boys will show them what the British bulldog is made of. These Huns are no match for the cream of the British Empire. They don't play cricket.' He rambled on for a few minutes before becoming incoherent and slumping forwards in his chair.

'So, what *do* you think will happen tomorrow?' asked Danny, pouring out more drinks for Freddie and himself.

'Daniel, old chap, we're going over the top to fight machine guns and heavy artillery armed with a stick and a popgun. I think there's a good chance we'll all be killed.'

'Well, that's put a dampener on things, ha, ha, ha, ha!' Tommy Banter had returned to the dugout to catch the end of the conversation. 'Scrounged some coffee off your brother, sir. No milk or sugar left though.'

'What do you think, Banter?' questioned Freddie.

'Sir?'

'The attack tomorrow?'

'Well, sir, the way I look at is this; all England is here, so if we break through the war could be over. Got to give it a try, sir.'

'And if we don't break through?'

'Then the war will go on,' broke in Danny philosophically, 'whether we are still here or not.'

The three men sat around for a while, as Renshaw snored loudly in his chair. 'Tell us one of your jokes, Tommy,' said Freddie, breaking the now-sombre mood.

Corporal Banter considered for a bit, then began, 'The secretary of state for war, Lord Kitchener, God rest his soul, goes to see the prime minister at the start of hostilities in 1914 and says, 'I need a million men.' Asquith replies 'Don't you think that would be a bit much for you, at your age, K?'

'Very amusing, I don't think, Banter,' observed Dangerfield snootily after an embarrassing pause, 'considering the poor chap's only been dead a few weeks. You're casting aspersions on one of our country's greatest heroes.'

Freddie remained silent for about 20 seconds then began to giggle like a girl, eventually roaring out loud, 'Ha, ha, ha, ha, ha, oh that's a good one, Tommy!' Danny, too, began to titter, then laugh out loud. Soon the two officers were convulsed with laughter, tears streaming down their faces.

Tommy stood about looking nonplussed. 'I didn't think it was that funny!'

The noise woke Renshaw from his stupor, and he too began chortling loudly in his manner, though clearly had not heard the joke. The three old school chums laughed and cried until their ribs ached. Then they just cried.

'You know what?' blubbed Freddie through the tears, 'It's been a real pleasure knowing you two.'

Tommy lit himself a cigarette and poured a mug of the foul, lukewarm coffee, without milk or sugar, or much coffee come to that, since most of it was recycled cocoa beans. Disconcerted somewhat by the strange behaviour of the officers he wandered out into the night. To the south the flashes from the British guns lit up the sky in rainbow-like colours, red, yellow and orange – like a giant firework display. He thought how beautiful it appeared in the night sky, still not quite fully dark, despite it hurling destruction on those poor bastards the other side of no man's land. He tried drinking some of the coffee from his cracked cup. It tasted bitter and sour. A few soldiers were on guard and leaning over the parapet. Tommy slowly sucked in his breath, feeling his chest tighten with apprehension. It was now after midnight, the first of July. It was a warm night, but a shiver ran down his back like a shock wave. His mouth suddenly felt dry, despite the tepid liquid he was swallowing. Even above the noise of the guns he could hear the drunken officers hooting from the dugout, roaring loudly once more at some other joke. He smiled to himself and wished he were 15 again and back with his old chums at Wickham Dale.

Tommy wandered about in the trench for a while, briefly acknowledging those men he knew with nothing more than a nod and wondering how many would still be alive at the end of the day. In a few hours, the great attack would begin, and he considered whether he would survive it. He could feel the fear growing inside him, spreading like a cancer. There was another brief lull in the firing and Tommy could clearly hear the officers down below again, laughing like girls and singing some bawdy song. He began to hum the tune to himself. Then the words came.

*Comrades, comrades, ever since they were boys.*

*Sharing each other's sorrows, sharing each other's joys...*

Then the guns started up again.

# 16 – THE BATTLE FOR GOMMECOURT

*Flex the muscles, all you worthy fellows,*
*Fight the fight until the memory mellows.*

JOHN BIGGLESWORTH – *Brave Hearts*

Part of the strategy for the mass offensive by the British Army on 1 July 1916 was a diversionary action to the north of the Somme sector against the fortified village of Gommecourt, the westernmost point of the planned offensive against the German line of trenches that ran from the North Sea to the Swiss border. The two units that were to join the attack at Gommecourt were the North Midland (46th) Division and the London (56th) Division, part of the VII Corps of the British Third Army under the command of Lieutenant General Sir Edmund Allenby. Their purpose was to pin down, as far as possible, German infantry and artillery that might otherwise be employed against the main British and French attacks in the Somme valley.

The London Division included the 168th Brigade which comprised, among others, the 10th Battalion (Sportsmen's), Royal London Regiment and the 7th/8th Battalions of the Middlesex Regiment that included subaltern Jack Bigglesworth and captains Dangerfield and Renshaw. Captain Freddie Wright-Herbert commanded C

Company of the 10th London, which was ordered to go 'over the top' at 7.30am His brother Jimmy was a subaltern in D Company, as was Will Fulton. None of these junior officers were more than 20 years of age.

The Londoners were regarded as one of the best Territorial divisions of the British Army and many of their battalions had seen action during 1915, though not the 10th, which was a new unit. With some foresight, a forward trench had been dug to within 200yds of the enemy (no man's land being up to 800yds wide in this sector) which greatly assisted the jumping-off point for the assault. Gommecourt and its surrounding fortifications formed a salient, or bulge, in the trench line. The plan was for the North Midlanders to attack from the north and the Londoners from the south. If successful, the two divisions would 'pinch off' the salient, join up behind the village and surround the garrison therein.

Freddie, like most junior officers, was never given the full picture. Though no great military strategist, even he had surmised that his battalion was little more than cannon fodder, to be sacrificed for the greater cause, and furthermore there was a gap of one mile between the Third and Fourth Armies which would leave both open to flanking movements in the event of an enemy counterattack.

Armed with nothing but his revolver and walking stick, Captain Wright-Herbert led his company out into no man's land at the given signal. The attack was an initial success, unlike that to the north, and in only a few minutes the German front-line trenches had been taken without excessive casualties. As the second, third and fourth waves poured forward behind them, the front companies moved on the enemy's second defensive line beyond the village itself. Here the attack halted to await the agreed link-up with the 46th Division. By mid-morning, however, the German artillery had homed in on both the attacking units following up and those now manning the captured trenches. Casualties had begun to mount and there was no sign of the North Midland Division.

'Piece of cake, so far,' joked Freddie, taking a swig from his hip flask as another shell burst nearby, causing everyone to duck apart from the officer.

'I think I've shit myself,' groaned Tommy Banter, wheezing heavily in the trench next to his commanding officer.

'Never mind, Banter, no one will notice in all this muck. We'll send your pants back for Matron to wash, eh? Anyone seen my brother?'

'He's a little way along, sir, in the next trench,' said Hutton, a heavily built sergeant with a bristling moustache.

'Jolly good then, chaps. We'll just wait for the 46th to turn up. God, it's quiet here! At least the Huns won't shell their own trenches. Think I'll have a smoke before the party starts up again.'

'Er... excuse me, sir,' gasped Tommy as another shell exploded 50yds away. 'It's hardly quiet and I don't think it's our own artillery shelling us!'

'Hmm,' mused the officer, 'on further consideration, you may not be wrong there, young fellow.'

'Will Fulton got hit. I saw him go down.'

'Jolly rotten luck,' observed Freddie with little or no feeling. 'He never did quite look the part in the army, you know. Always funked the really fast bowling.'

'Excuse me again, sir, but shouldn't we get out of here? I don't think things are quite going to plan,' enquired the corporal with more than a hint of desperation in his voice.

'Nonsense!' barked Wright-Herbert, 'Everything's going swimmingly. The 46th'll be here in a jiffy. Don't be such a wet blanket.'

Tommy sank back into the wet duckboards and started to sing in a weedy, frightened voice.

*I want to go home...*

Just then, Freddie's brother came running up, hot and bothered.

'Jimmy, old boy, good to see you. What's the story?'

'Not good, Freddie,' The younger sibling was breathless and covered in mud. 'The 46th are pinned down. Some of them haven't even made their first objective. Didn't even get 50 yards. We're stuck here on our own with no more reserves coming up. The Middlesex boys really copped it getting up. There's Huns in the trenches further over. I reckon we've lost nearly half our strength already.'

*... take me back over the sea... where the Alleyman can't get at me...*

'What's up with him?' asked Jimmy, staring at Tommy's hunched figure.

Freddie ignored the question but instead asked one of his own. 'Any orders?'

*O my, I don't want to die...*

'I've sent runners back to brigade,' Jimmy reported, 'but none of them have returned. It's murder out there! Most of the officers of the 10th are dead or wounded. Colonel Vaughan was hit barely out of our trench. They've got our number all right. You're the most senior officer I've found so far.'

'Oh shit!' moaned Tommy. Murder is exactly what it is, he thought. 'What do we do now?'

*I want to go home…*

'Well, we'd better try and push on,' suggested Freddie. 'No point staying here like sitting ducks. We must try and link up with any elements of the 46th that might have got through. Send any officers you can find to me here.'

'I think Jack Bigglesworth made it over with some of the Middlesex boys, but not many others, I fear.' He noticed Tommy slumped at the bottom of the trench. 'I see Banter's not laughing so much these days.'

'Dangerfield and Renshaw?'

Jimmy shook his head sadly. 'No.'

*… we're 'ere because we're 'ere… because we're 'ere… because we're 'ere…*

Freddie looked pensive for a moment and, showing no emotion, lit his pipe again as his brother disappeared around the bend of the trench. A few moments later an exhausted-looking Jack Bigglesworth came running up.

'Ah, Bigglesworth, pleased to see you. What price this?'

'The devil to pay!' panted the junior officer. 'Our boys got caught out in the open. The Boche guns homed in on us before we even got to the forward trench. Most of the officers are down. What's that terrible smell!'

'Corporal Banter's soiled his pants in a funk,' laughed Private Bell, a young soldier looking no more than 16. Anyone got any toilet paper?'

*... send for the boys of the girls' brigade... to set old England free...*

'Shut up, Banter! Right then,' ordered Freddie, 'Bigglesworth, you stay here with 10 men and secure this position.' I'll go forward with the rest of the chaps until we meet up with the Midland boys. Get the lads to collect as many cricket balls as we've got for a bombing party. I'll push upwards towards the village.'

*... send for me mother, me sister and me brother, but for gawd's sake don't send me...*

'I think we should go back, sir,' said Jack. 'We're sticking out here like a sore thumb and it won't be long before the whole German artillery gets our bearings. Their infantry is already massing for a counterattack and...'

'Enough!' yelled Freddie. 'I'm in command here and our orders are to press on until we link up with the 46th. Hobbs, Fry, lead the way with grenades. First sign of Fritz you bowl a full toss in their direction. Banter, you're with me.'

Just then a terrible, piercing shriek rent the air around them followed by a huge explosion a few yards outside the trench. Giant clods of earth, accompanied by what seemed like flesh and blood, were spewed into the air showering the British soldiers and making a gruesome splash on their helmets.

Tommy vomited as he was hit by the human debris and started to warble again in his tinny voice.

*... Goodbye Piccadilly... farewell Leicester Square...*

'Tommy can't make it, Freddie,' pleaded Jack. 'Look at him, he's off his head!'

'Was he ever anything else!' laughed his captain. 'Get him moving!'

Tommy Banter squatted at the bottom of the trench, curled up in the foetal position.

*... It's a long way to Tipperary... but my heart is there...*

Freddie gazed at his batman for a few seconds then drew a deep sigh and turned to Jack. 'All right, keep an eye on him. I'm going for a recce.' With that he disappeared round the bend of the trench, followed by a few willing soldiers.

Presently another shell burst nearby, sending more clods of earth flying up into the sky. 'Oh fuck, I've shit myself again!' wailed Tommy.

'Don't worry, old chap,' Jack commiserated. 'I pissed my pants when we were crossing no man's land. Compton! Jessop! take one bend in the trench each and sing out if you spot any Huns.' He slid down and sat on the duckboards next to his quivering old pal.

'Fuck this for a game of soldiers!' complained Tommy.

'Thomas, my old chum, you've no idea how profound that statement was.'

'Have you got a fag?' the corporal asked after a while.

'Afraid not, old boy.' Tommy's request briefly made Jack think of Kitty and the cigarette case, which he had given to her after their recent parting. 'Tell you what though...' He pulled out a small flask from his jacket and handed it to Tommy, who took a large gulp, nearly choking.

'Fuck me sideways, Jack!' he spluttered. 'What's that stuff?'

'Schnapps. The Huns make it out of old potatoes, so I believe. Got it off one of their prisoners in exchange for some plum and apple jam.'

Yet another explosion, this time even closer. The mad din of war was getting louder. 'They've got our number alright.' confirmed Jack. 'We're right up bally creek without a paddle now. How did it all come to this, Tommy old son? I wish I'd gone up to university now instead of volunteering for this madness.'

'You know what?' Tommy said, 'We should get the hell out of here now. That fucking bastard Freddie is going to get us all killed. He thinks he's still on the cricket field, thinks he can win the war all by himself!'

# 17 – THE CORNER
# OF A FOREIGN FIELD

*Through fire and rain, through joy and pain*
*The old school shall prevail.*
*The bloom of youth, the sacred truth*
*The ghosts of Wickham Dale.*

School Song

For a moment, the bombardment around Gommecourt seemed to ease, but it was merely an illusion.

Tommy asked, 'Anyone had any news of Billy, lately?'

'Last I heard,' replied Jack, 'the bounder landed himself a plum staff job at HQ. Probably making the tea and running errands for Allenby.'

'He always was a lucky bastard, falling on his feet. I heard Will Fulton bought it though.'

'No!'

'One minute he was running along nicely, the next he was arse-end up in some shell hole.'

'Poor old Willow.'

'He might have just tripped up and fallen over though, ha, ha, ha, ha!'

'That's it, Tommy, keep your pecker up,' After a pause Jack asked, 'You know, there's one thing I never understood. What really happened with that goat, the cucumber and the sticking plaster?'

Before Tommy could answer there came the sound of nearby gunfire and another explosion. Private Fry, blood pouring from a gaping wound in his head, came staggering round the bend of the trench, closely followed by Captain Wright-Herbert. 'Aye, aye,' said Jack, hurriedly getting to his feet, 'it's all on for young and old now.' Tommy seemed to cringe back into his shell and started warbling once more.

*Mademoiselle from Armanteers... parley-vous...*

Freddie came stumbling up, gasping for breath. 'No way through. Boche everywhere. Looks like we're on a proper sticky wicket this time.' Private Peterson, a huge man with a shaven head followed, carrying a limp Jimmy Wright-Herbert.

*... Mademoiselle from Armanteers... parley-vous...*

'Jimmy's got a Blighty one, lucky devil, not too serious.'

'Freddie, we've got to get out of here, otherwise we'll be surrounded!' shouted Jack.

*... Mademoiselle from Armanteers... hasn't been fucked for forty years... inky-pinky parley-vous...*

'For God's sake, shut up, Banter!' Freddie pulled his binoculars up to his face and scanned the horizon in the direction of the village. 'You're right, Lieutenant, but we've had no orders to retire. Sergeant Willis, is that machine-gun unit still with us?'

'Yes, sir.'

'Right, get them over here on the double.' More shells shrieked overhead, raining debris down into the trench. Within seconds a horrific scream was heard from the next section.

'At least get the wounded out,' pleaded Jack as the smoke cleared.

'Alright, alright,' agreed the senior officer after some thought. 'I'll stay here with the machine-gunners until everyone gets clear.'

'It's fucking miles back to our lines!' whined Tommy.

'I'll order a hansom cab for you, shall I, Banter?' There was more of a hint of sarcasm in Freddie's voice. 'You're bloody useless, always were! Never thought I'd see a Widdler play the coward. Bigglesworth, get him out of my sight! He can carry Jimmy back. Might even win himself a VC.'

'What about me?'

Freddie looked long and hard at the junior officer, the strain beginning to show on his blackened face. 'All right, you go too and take what's left of the battalion. Mine as well.'

'And the machine-gun section?'

Freddie turned away, lifting the binoculars to his eyes again in the direction of the advancing enemy. 'Everyone can go except Bowes, Foster and Verity. They can stay with me.'

'What about you?'

'I'm the skipper, ain't I? Got to hold the innings together until stumps. Anyway, reinforcements will be here soon. I'll hold them until you get clear.'

Jack failed to grasp the analogy. He stared at his former school captain, his great schoolboy hero, with an anxious face, his tired heart pounding. He was sweating in the hot afternoon sun and his muddy uniform was soaked, stale and fetid. Tears began to form in his stinging eyes, his body feeling so stiff he could hardly move. 'There are no reserves, skipper. Everyone is up. Everything that's due to come up. We're on our own. I know that. You know that. You've always known that. We're expendable.'

Freddie regarded Jack with a grim expression, smiling through the caked mud, but did not reply. 'You're wounded!' said Jack, seeing blood trickling down the arm of his captain's uniform.

'Oh, it's only a scratch, old boy. Nothing to worry about. Matron will patch me up.' He seemed to be amused by the thought. 'Now run along, there's a good chap.'

Jack hesitated for a moment, indecision that could have been fatal. In the distance he heard the incessant pounding of an enemy machine gun. Some of the sandbags at the top of the trench exploded with the impact of high velocity bullets. 'You don't have to stay here, Freddie. We've done our duty, followed our orders, gained our objectives. It's not our fault the 46th haven't made it. The plan was flawed anyway. We all knew that. There's no point staying here to get killed or captured. Why do you have to play the bloody hero all the time!'

'I told you get going, and it's 'sir' to you, Bigglesworth!' It was the only the second time Jack had seen Freddie so angry. The previous time was when he was wrongly given out leg before by Jesse James in the Wankeen Cup.

'Matron's not here, Freddie. You know Renshaw and Dangerfield didn't make it. There's nobody left.' Freddie said nothing. Jack was becoming increasingly angry and frustrated. He knew if Freddie stayed there was no way back for him. 'Why does it all have to end like this?'

The captain closed his eyes, looked down to the ground and sighed. 'And your point is, what?'

'The school, Weston House, the 1st XI!' Tears were running down Jack's face and mingling with the mud and powder stains on his hot cheeks.

'What are you blathering on about, Bigglesworth? You always were an old woman, having to be a stickler for something or other.' Freddie's face was set hard with determination. 'Now listen to me, Lieutenant. The Wickham Dale Cricket XI existed long before you and I were even thought about and will live on long after the likes of us are dust in the earth. Now for God's sake, do as you are ordered!'

'Is that an order, sir!'

'Yes, it damned well is, now fetch off before I have you court-martialled for insubordination!'

Jack did as he was told. Reluctantly he grabbed Tommy by the shoulders and pulled him to his feet. 'Right, Corporal Banter, give Lieutenant Wright-Herbert a hand. Corporal Hirst, round up what's left of the battalion. We're getting out of here.'

They waited for another lull in the bombardment, then hauled themselves back out of the enemy trench and into the open fields. Jack was the last to leave. He looked back to where Freddie stood, resolute as ever, awaiting his fate. He tried to call out to him one last time, but this throat was now so dry no words would come out.

'Sir, we have to go,' pleaded Hirst, 'Please, sir!'

With tears streaming down his face, Jack turned away and began to move back towards the British lines.

*

With bullets and ordnance flying around them the shattered remnants of the 56th Division retreated as best they could as the sun slowly began to fall from the sky and already almost obliterated by the smoke of a thousand guns.

Corporal Tommy Banter, carrying Lieutenant Jimmy Wright-Herbert on his shoulders, staggered from one shell hole to another across the 800yds of open country. Somewhere, perhaps close, perhaps in the distance, the stuttering of a machine gun could be heard. Then suddenly a hot wind of bullets and screaming shells began to rain down on the retreating battalions with men, tired, hungry, exhausted and parched with thirst, starting to fall.

Jack Bigglesworth stumbled along, crouched almost on all fours, sometimes staggering forwards, sometimes glancing back, desperately trying to keep the survivors together, every fresh explosion causing his bowels to discharge into his britches. He was amazed that there was anything left! They had almost made it back to the British forward trench when another massive explosion tore the ground from beneath their feet. Jack was hurled into the air, landing with a thump in a shell hole. At first, he thought he must be dead, for he could perceive nothing but a bright orange light and a thunderous ringing in his ears. The wind had been blown from his already fatigued body and he lay motionless apart from his chest heaving with painful spasms. Then everything went deathly quiet until he heard the awful sound of a man screaming in pain.

Slowly, Jack looked about him, but could see nothing but smoke. His ears were so painful that all he could hear was a loud ringing. 'Biggles,' cried a weak voice from what seemed a million miles away. 'Biggles, help me, for God's sake. Oh Mother!' As the smoke cleared Bigglesworth pulled himself up. On the other side of the shell hole, half submerged in filthy water, was Tommy Banter, sitting up, his arms dangling limply at his sides and blood dribbling from his open mouth. Lying next to him was the limp body of Jimmy Wright-Herbert. Another soldier he did not recognise was slowly rising from the water, a bloody gash in his cheek. 'Biggles, I'm dying!' came a barely familiar voice.

His body aching in every bone, Jack dragged himself across the morass. 'Who's there?' he demanded of the unknown soldier.

'Private Grace, sir, 7th Middlesex.'

'Are you badly hurt?'

'No, sir,' groaned the soldier, an odd humming noise buzzing in the air. 'Still in one piece I think.'

'Tommy, are you alright?'

'Think I've bought it, Biggles. O sweet Jesus' came the unfamiliar voice. 'Hurts like fuck!'

'Where are you hit?'

'Fucking everywhere!' Full of fucking holes, that's poor old Tommy Banter.'

'He's still breathing alright, sir,' observed Grace, a huge man with a thick ginger moustache. Beside him, Lieutenant

Wright-Herbert let out a long moan. 'Officer still alive too, sir.' Another shell exploded nearby, showering the soldiers with more clods of earth and splinters of wood.

Jack dragged himself up alongside the other three men. His leg hurt like hell, but he could see no obvious wound. 'Can you get up, Grace?'

'Think so, sir. Just a head wound.' Despite his size, the man had a weedy, almost feminine voice.

'Let's get out of here then.'

'Sorry, Jack, I'm a goner,' whispered Tommy. 'This fucking fucker's fucking fucked.'

'Now look, old boy, you're not all that bad. We're all going to be ok,' Jack was less optimistic than he sounded. 'However, I must say your language has deteriorated somewhat since you left school. I don't know what Professor Purviss would make of it all.'

'Beg pardon, sir,' Grace pointed out, 'but I don't think there's much danger of us leavin' 'ere at the present. Pop our 'eads up above this 'ole and mos' likely get 'em blown orf, sure as eggs are eggs. Best wait till it gets dark an' take our chances then.'

'Yes, you're right,' sighed Jack, annoyed that he had not thought straight himself. He felt bruised and battered but could see no obvious wounds, although blood was seeping from his ears. He reached inside his uniform and pulled out a hip flask. 'Listen, Tommy, if you can face up to Pongo Smelling you can get away with this... Well, bugger me with a broomstick, brush end first!'

'What is it?'

Jack pulled the flask out from his torn pocket, but the metal was buckled and twisted, a large hot piece of shrapnel embedded in it. 'My mother always said I should never drink, but this old tin can has saved my life, I reckon!'

'Any left, sir?' asked Grace hopefully.

Jack inspected the wreckage. 'Afraid not, old boy.'

'Water!' cried Tommy.

'No water either, old chap,' croaked Jack, 'unless you want to drink that bilge you're sitting in!'

Tommy laid back in the filth and gasped in pain. 'I'm sorry if I've ever been rotten to you in the past, Jack.' Nobody had the strength to speak, and the mayhem appeared to calm for a while. 'How's Mr W-H doing?'

'I think 'e's still with us,' said Grace, adding, 'at least for now.'

'Try not to move, Tommy.'

'Chance'll be a fine thing, owww!'

'I can't believe it's all going to end like this,' moaned Jack. 'I wished I believed in God.' He thought of his mother, of Kitty, of schooldays.

'Even 'e couldn't get us out of this mess, sir.'

'Where are we? Our forward trench can't be far, but in which direction?'

'Beggin' pardon, sir,' said Grace, 'but our lines must be to the west, in the direction of the settin' sun, which if I ain't mistaken is, er, that way.'

The private pointed in the direction they were facing. A groan of agony came from somewhere nearby outside the hole. Jack could just about make out the sun in the distance through the smoky haze. He quietly cursed himself again for not seeing this and for being shown up by a simple Tommy. They would have to sit it out until dark, which was still many hours away.

# 18 – A RICHER DUST CONCEALED

*The death of one man is a tragedy.*
*The death of millions is a statistic.*

JOSEPH STALIN

Time passed slowly. The exhausted soldiers sat uncomfortably in the stinking pool, thinking, wondering, worrying. A machine gun was still hammering away somewhere and, judging by the occasional scream or wail of pain, finding targets. The hole stank of mud, blood, shit and piss and the air around was thick with the acrid smell of cordite and explosive, but there was nothing for them to do but wait it out.

'Tommy, are you still conscious?' It was almost dark now and Jack deduced it to be around 9pm; his pocket watch had not survived the day. The tumult seemed to have died down although red flares split the sky every few minutes. Periodically, but less often than before, the machine gun barked out its hail of death.

'I'm still bleeding like a stuffed pig, ouch!' came a hoarse response. 'I'm so cold and thirsty.' Tommy's voice sounded weaker than before, and his breathing was erratic.

'I think you'll find it's a *stuck* pig, sir.' Grace's pedantry was beginning to annoy Jack.

'Quiet! I heard something. Grace, have you still got your rifle?'

'Yes, sir.'

'Stick your head over the top and see what it is and keep your head down.'

'Sir'

Slowly, the private slithered up to the top of the shell hole, peered about, then slid down into the muck again. 'It's a stretcher party, sir.'

'Anywoon ther?' came a booming northern voice.

'Be careful, sir,' warned Grace, tightly gripping his rifle. 'It could be a trick.'

A face appeared over the side of the depression, belonging to a big man with a Red Cross band around his arm. 'It's al reet, brass 'ave negotiated armistice with Alleyman. 'Ow many of ye?'

'Four,' said Jack, 'Two gravely wounded.'

'Reet, I'll tek woon, two o' you buggers tek outher. We'll get stretcher over 'ere in a jiffy.'

'Do you know what RAMC stands for?' whispered Grace, when the man was out of earshot.

'Royal Army Medical Corps.'

'No – Rob All My Comrades. I don't trust these bastards. They'd 'ave the shit out your arse if they thought they could sell it.'

'Well, that's comforting to know, Grace. I'm sure they are not all like that.'

'Just be careful, sir.'

Nevertheless, with great care, the two soldiers hauled Tommy to his feet, causing him to groan in agony, loud enough to alert anyone close by.

'Keep it darn, chum,' said the orderly. 'Theers always a few snipers that's got no conscience.'

He was right. Hardly had the man lifted Jimmy out of the hole and followed the other three, than shots rang out. One spat across the ground, grazing Jack's foot.

'Fookin' 'ell!' yelled the RAMC man, 'Theers fookin' armistice, you basteds!' It mattered little, as the British lines were only 30yds away. In an undignified heap all five men tumbled into the forward trench as more bullets came singing over the parapet. Tommy screamed with pain again as he fell into the mud.

'Thank you,' said Jack to the big man. 'What's your name?'

'Barlow, sir.'

'Thank you, Barlow. Are you going out again?'

'Ave to, sir.' An explosion came nearby. 'Bin oop an' darn al' day.' More bullets came humming over the trench. 'Fookin' basteds! German coonts!' Barlow disappeared back into no man's land.

'He's a brave man,' Jack said.

'Leave me here,' moaned Tommy, 'I can't go any further.'

'I'm not leaving you. We're almost home now. Matron'll patch you up. We'll soon have you back opening the batting.'

Tommy began to murmur a tune again.

*I don't want a bayonet in me belly...*

'What's that, old chap?' croaked Jack.

'He's delirious, sir,' Grace said. 'Barlow gave 'im a dose o' morphine. Probably can't feel a thing. You hop off, sir. I'll take care of 'im.'

*... I don't want me bollocks shot away...*

'No, I'll stay with him.' Jack's throat was so dry and sore he could hardly speak. He had never felt so weary. Thanks, private, get that head wound seen to.'

'I'll take the other officer then, sir. His needs seem the greater if that's all right with you.'

'Yes, yes, run along.'

*... I'd rather stay in England, merry, merry England... an' fornicate me bleedin' life away.*

'Wouldn't we all, Thomas, wouldn't we all.' Too tired to move, Jack slumped to the bottom of the trench. His aching arm moved to the top pocket of his jacket and took out the little photograph of Kitty he kept there, but it crumbled to pieces in his hand, and he started to cry uncontrollably.

But Tommy Banter didn't hear. He had slipped away into blessed unconsciousness.

*

On 1 July 1916, 14 divisions of the British Army plus five of the French, a total of 150,000 men, had stood ready to attack the German line in the valley of the River Somme over a front of some 18 miles. For seven days and seven nights the British guns, light and heavy, had pounded the enemy defences, the greatest artillery barrage in the history of warfare. It had seemed that nothing could live through such a bombardment of fire and steel. Yet when the infantry left their trenches on that sunny morning, they were mown down by machine guns and blown to bits by artillery shells. Those that did reach the German lines found that, in some places, the barbed wire was still intact.

By the end of the day the 'Butcher's Bill' – the list of British casualties – officially stood at 19,240 dead (or later died of wounds), 35,493 wounded, 2,152 missing and 585 prisoners in enemy hands – a total of 57,470 men lost, almost exactly half of the soldiers in the 143 battalions that had gone 'over the top' on that day were listed as casualties. Only one in four officers who had bravely led out their men over no man's land remained uninjured. The total British losses on that fateful day were the equivalent of 75 battalions, or six full divisions of fighting infantry. There were two casualties for every yard of British front line. Unsurprisingly, the first day of the Somme battle was the worst disaster in the history of British arms. Even the carnage on the day of Waterloo had incurred only 8,234 British casualties.

The London (56th) Division at Gommecourt had suffered more than most. From the seven battalions that had taken part in the attack, over 1,700 men had been killed, some 200 or so were prisoners of war and a further 2,300 had been wounded, many of them still awaiting rescue or attention. Fortunately, that evening, a short armistice had been agreed with the local German commander and many of them, including Tommy Banter and Jimmy Wright-Herbert, had been saved. The Division had carried out every task to which it had been assigned; it had taken the entire enemy front-line trench system and had reached and taken the second line of defences behind the village of Gommecourt, but the failure of the North Midland Division to the north of the salient had left the 56th stranded and eventually cut off. They had lost everything gained, fought with the upmost gallantry and suffered grievously for no eventual territorial gain.

No battalion had been decimated more than the 10th Sportsmen's. Of the 864 fighting men employed in the assault, just 122 remained fit for duty on 2 July. Every one of its company commanders was either dead, wounded or missing. The carnage among the junior officers in all units was so devastating that Second Lieutenant Jack Bigglesworth found himself second-in-command of a Middlesex battalion company. To his great surprise and relief, he discovered that Will Fulton, believed to have fallen in the fray, was in fact still alive. A bullet had hit him full in the chest, but most of the impact had been absorbed by his faithful copy of the Wisden Cricket Almanac that he always carried in his breast pocket. Cricket had saved his life. Along with Tommy Banter and Jimmy Wright-Herbert he had been taken to the nearest dressing station and thence onward to a field hospital. Others were not so fortunate.

Jack Bigglesworth was officially relieved of duty on 3 July, suffering from battle trauma, but was back in the line a week later. Undeterred, the British attacked again and a night assault later in July was partially successful. But it was not followed up and the stalemate continued. For four more months the two sides slogged away at each other as the casualties mounted. Even the new secret weapon, the tank, could not affect a breakthrough, the great machines proving too cumbersome and liable to break down. Eventually the battle petered out in the mud and cold of November, with no significant gain. Britain's citizen army had fought its first battle, and was slowly learning the art of mechanised war, but at a fearful cost. The conflict would not end in 1916. Many feared it could not end in 1917 and that the slaughter would go on relentlessly.

*

Meanwhile, back at Wickham Dale College, all hell had broken loose in a series of scandals that rocked the school to its very foundations. In the late summer of 1916, Matron Olive Blackwell had been caught *in flagrante delicto* with a young girl, purporting to be her daughter, in a hotel room in Brighton. The girl in question was none other than her nursing assistant Emily Dickens. Summoned before a tribunal of school governors Miss Dickens spilled the beans. Only then did the full scale of Matron Blackwell's depravity final emerge.

As a child, Olive had been abused by her soldier stepfather. After his death she had cared for her sick mother for many years before, on the old woman's passing, she obtained the position of Matron at the school, under the sponsorship of her brother, a serving master at the college. Seemingly a popular and much-loved member of staff, it transpired that for many years she had taken advantage of her position by indulging in sexual perversity with many of the students in her care, including masturbating the younger boys, acts of fellatio and even penetrative intercourse with some of the more mature pupils.

Olive at first denied the accusations, then declared that she was only 'making the boys feel loved as they were away from home and missing their mothers'. In a desperate attempt to save herself, she threatened to blackmail headmaster Alistair Hughes and reveal the details of their long-standing liaison if he did not stand up for her. Hughes refused, denying everything and citing alcoholism and instability as the reason for her desperate and damaging accusations. He would have got away with it had it not been for the testimony of Emily Dickens, who had been witness to episodes of the couple's sordid activities. Matron and headmaster were arbitrarily dismissed. When staff and pupils returned to school in the autumn of 1916, they found themselves with a new headmaster and matron. To escape the ensuing scandal Emily joined the RAMC as a trainee nurse and was posted to France.

Fortunately for the school, news of the disgrace had broken during the summer holidays and for the most part had been hushed up, though not surprisingly rumours abounded for some time, particularly among the masters. Jeremy Brooman was the main beneficiary of Hughes's fall, being appointed to the headmastership in his place.

The new principal had only been at the helm for a few months when an even more damaging obloquy threatened to further tarnish the school's standing. The English master, Professor Cornelius Perviss, had for many years been indulging in his own secret vice, which involved luring unsuspecting boys to his study on the pretext of punishment, forcing them to drop their trousers and bend over his desk for a caning, and then sodomising them. If any boy complained, he was threatened with even worse punishment. Perviss said quite brazenly that it would be their word against his and that no one would believe them. Finally, one brave student told his parents of what had occurred. Emboldened by the accusations, other boys came forward to testify against Perviss's evil exploits, including former pupils who had left formal education many years before. This time there could be no whitewash. Perviss was dismissed and died in ignominy just a few months later.

Poor Brooman was saddled with salvaging what was left of the college's reputation. It was hard enough for him that over 200 former pupils had already fallen in the war. Now, suddenly, well-to-do families no longer wished to send their sons to such a sink of iniquity. For a while it seemed the school might even have to close, but the new headmaster's hard work to restore Wickham Dale's honour slowly began to pay dividends.

# 19 – SWEET WINE OF YOUTH

*Play the tune, piper, and watch them all follow*
*To the slaughter in their new world*
*And corners of foreign fields*

JOHN BIGGLESWORTH – *The Lofty Shade Advances*

It was a lovely summer's day in late July and the garden of the Ketteridge residence was looking its best. Hilda Ketteridge had been fussing about, pruning and collecting cuttings for the house. After the death of her only son, she had kept herself busy, trying desperately to forget her terrible heartbreak and sorrow. Her husband was at work, but her daughter Kitty was home on a few days' leave from her Women's Land Army exertions. For a moment, the war seemed a long way off.

After a while Hilda breezed into the sitting-room through the French windows and sat down in a heap, perspiring slightly. She was a plump woman in her late 40s with a ruddy face and thick black hair like her daughter, though it was greying slightly at the temples. 'Ooh, I'm all puffed out,' she gasped, 'It's so warm out there. Kitty, be a darling and ask Withers to rustle up some lemon tea.'

Her daughter was standing by the mantelpiece, lighting a cigarette. 'Sorry, Mother,' she murmured, seeming distracted. These days she wore her hair in a bun at the back of her head, and dressed in rough, simple clothes.

'Oh Kitty, smoking is an awful habit for a young girl. If your father could see you now. Honestly, I don't know. I suppose you picked that up from your farming friends.'

'Oh Mummy, I'm not a girl, and don't be such a hypocrite. I've seen you do it.' Kitty sighed, still appearing distant.

'The odd one after dinner perhaps, when your father isn't looking. Is everything alright, darling? You seem a bit far off and you are not looking well.' Hilda rang the bell herself to summon their butler.

'I'm just a bit tired. I had a letter from Johnny this morning.' Kitty wandered to the French windows and gazed out into the garden.

Hilda asked, 'He's alive and well?'

Kitty drew another deep sigh. 'He's alive.' She wandered back into the room and sat down. 'I've been so worried. He survived the big attack, but a lot of his friends were killed.'

'Oh, darling, I'm so sorry. Is he alright?'

Kitty sighed again. 'Just about, I suppose.' Withers, the family's venerable retainer, bumbled into the room with a tray and put it down on the table. Hilda ushered him away.

'Tea, darling?'

'No thank you,' Kitty replied, 'I think I'll have a drink instead.'

'It's a bit early for that, isn't it?' queried her mother, disapproval in her voice. Kitty walked to the drinks cabinet and poured herself a large whisky, then added a squirt of soda from a siphon.

'Goodness! Are you drinking whisky now?'

'Oh, Mummy, stop fussing. Johnny drinks it.'

'Johnny.' Hilda repeated evenly. 'So, what did he have to say then?'

'The attack was a disaster. Thousands of our poor boys have been killed.'

'But the newspaper reports said it had gone quite well and...'

'Oh Mother, you don't believe everything you read in the papers, do you? Half of it is lies and the rest propaganda.'

'Well, I don't know what to believe any more. Oh, darling, do sit down and have some tea. I can't stand you hovering around.'

Kitty ignored her. 'Johnny says the newspapers only print an economy of the truth. The true reality is always concealed from us, lest it be bad for morale.' She walked back to the mantelpiece and stubbed out her cigarette, then sat down with a bump on the leather settee. Johnny's silver cigarette case was lying on the coffee table. Kitty picked it up and unconsciously turned it over and over in her hands.

'Where did you get that?' asked her mother.

'Johnny gave it to me. It belonged to a fellow officer who was killed.' Kitty took a cigarette out of the case and began tapping it on the lid, then absently put it in her mouth.

Johnny again, thought Hilda. 'It all sounds a bit mawkish to me. Oh Kitty, if you must smoke, at least use a cigarette holder. It's so undignified. You look like some common hussy in a cheap saloon bar.'

'Oh, for God's sake, Mother, stop bloody well lecturing me!' Kitty flared, throwing the cigarette down on the table, rising and striding to the drinks cabinet where she poured herself another whisky, without bothering with any soda this time. She took a deep gulp of the fiery liquid, almost choking as it burned the back of her throat.

Briefly she felt a little giddy. For a moment neither woman spoke. Hilda busied herself with the teacups then broke the silence. 'I really don't know what has become of you, Catherine. You take no care in your appearance, smoke cigarettes, drink whisky, swear like a trooper. You're so angry and sullen all the time.'

'Anything else? I must be such a disappointment to you.' When her mother called her by her given name Kitty knew she was in trouble.

'No of course you're not, darling, but you used to be such a sweet little girl.'

'Oh, mother,' Kitty sighed, 'I was never a sweet little girl. You obviously didn't pay much attention to me.'

'Well, I suppose you always had a bit of a temper on you,' Hilda replied, bewildered by her daughter's strange behaviour.

'Now you remember.'

'It's this bloody war!' Kitty continued after a pause. 'It's changed everybody and everything.'

'Honestly, I don't know, as if your father and I haven't got enough to cope with, your poor brother still warm in his grave.'

'He's not in a grave,' Kitty stated without emotion. 'They never found his body.'

Hilda put her head in her hands and began to cry. 'Oh, you cruel, heartless girl.'

'Oh, do stop snivelling, Mother, and face up to the truth. Those incompetent generals and politicians are systematically killing off the best of this male generation and no one dares say anything about it!'

Hilda blew her nose and tried to be brave. Her daughter's brazen attitude frightened her, but she refused to be intimidated. 'You have never been the same since you started mixing with those common Land Army girls. You even dress like one.'

'Well, at least I'm doing something practical,' Kitty observed sardonically, 'unlike your women's organisations and their silly food parcels.'

'They're not silly,' Hilda sniffed. 'Our boys at the front need cheering up.'

Kitty stopped pacing about and looked at her mother shrinking in her seat. 'It's men and munitions the army needs, not cigarettes, nerve tonic and... and... plum and apple jam!'

Another pregnant silence followed. Kitty relented for a moment and sat down next to her mother. 'Look, Mummy, I don't mean to sound callous. I know how upset you have been about Julian. We all have.'

'I don't recall you shedding any tears over him.' Hilda stared disapprovingly at her daughter, trying to make sense of her.

'No, but then he was always your favourite, wasn't he? You and Daddy doted on him. I was just an afterthought. You couldn't wait to pack me off to that awful boarding school.'

'Oh, darling, that's not true.' Hilda took her daughter's hand in hers. 'We have always loved you.'

'Well, you had a funny way of showing it.'

'Oh, darling!'

Kitty slipped her hand away and stood up, walked over to the mantelpiece, sipped her drink and breathed deeply. 'It doesn't matter. Everything will be different now. We women are doing things we would never have been allowed to do in peacetime, taking over all the dirty jobs while our men are at the front. When the war is over the government must give us the vote and we will all be emancipated. Then we can even stand for parliament. I might even become a politician myself.'

'Don't be ridiculous!'

Kitty struck a match and lit another cigarette. 'It's not ridiculous! In your world we would be good for nothing but flower arranging and embroidery. Don't you think we women could do a better job of running the country than these warmongers and profiteers who are in charge now?'

Hilda was becoming more and more agitated at the direction the conversation was taking, so changed the subject. 'It really is about time you settled down, darling. We must find you a nice, steady young man, especially if you are set on not going to university now. What about that Bruce Hillingdon, the nice boy who works with your father? He was very taken with you.'

'I don't like him. He makes my flesh crawl! Anyway, why is he sitting at a comfortable desk in the Foreign Office when he should be out at the front doing his bit? Now the government has brought in conscription, all the cowards and slackers will have to go!'

'Ha! now *you* are sounding like a politician!' Hilda was fighting back. 'Listen to yourself. A moment ago, you were complaining about all your contemporaries being slaughtered and now you can't wait to send them out to the war!'

Kitty started pacing nervously about the room, pulling on her cigarette, her mother looking on evermore disapprovingly. 'Johnny says we all have to fight this war together, to the death, if necessary, until the enemy is beaten. It's the only way we are going to win.'

Hilda finally lost her temper. 'Johnny says this, Johnny says that! Johnny, Johnny, Johnny, Johnny! You talk of nothing else!'

'What of it! He's the only person in the world I really care about!'

'Oh, Catherine!' Hilda was close to tears again. 'How can you say that to your own mother?'

'Because it's true!'

'You only want him because you know you can twist him round your little finger. You were always getting that poor boy into trouble with your wilfulness.'

'Maybe, but he's a gentle soul who would never harm a fly, yet he's out there risking his life fighting for our freedom so we can all live in peace again. He may have to kill someone he has never seen. He is afraid, but he's not a coward. He has so much fortitude!' Kitty was on the verge of tears herself now, tears of anger. She had never felt so exasperated with her mother.

Another silence followed, then Hilda plucked up the courage to ask a question she did not really want to know the answer to. 'Have you ever spoken of marriage?'

Kitty was at the French windows again, letting the warm summer breeze wash over her. 'No,' she said after a while, 'but if he asked me, I would say yes.'

'Oh, Catherine, he's totally unsuitable and you know it! He is such a dull dog and his family have no real money these days. Worst of all, he's a dreamer; all those silly poems.'

Kitty was angrier than ever now as she turned to face her mother. 'I don't care! I love him. I shall be 21 soon and can marry whomever I please and there's nothing you can do about it!'

'Love! Love!' Hilda spat the word out as if it was a disease. 'What does a girl like you know about love?'

'More than you think!'

Hilda stood up, startled. 'What do you mean by that? What have you done?' Kitty bit her tongue and did not reply. 'Catherine, is there something you ought to tell me? You're not in trouble, are you?'

'No, of course not!' Kitty wanted to spite her silly mother, tell her the guilty secret she harboured. Thinking better of it, she kept silent and walked out into the garden.

*

The war dragged inevitably and remorselessly on. Combined efforts of the Allies in 1916 – Russians, Italians, French and British – failed to make any significant progress against the Central Powers. In 1917 the French army mutinied, their soldiers worn down and sick of futile, thoughtless offensives, directed by incompetent generals, that only ended in defeat and destruction. The Americans entered the fight, but it would be another year before their forces could be effective on the Western Front. The onus to carry on the war then fell almost entirely on the British.

In the summer of 1917, they attacked once more in the Ypres sector of southern Belgium, but the appalling August weather bogged down the assault and the battlefield became a sea of mud. The advance finally floundered on the Passchendaele ridge. A further quarter of a million soldiers were lost for no great territorial gain.

In the autumn of 1917 the Russians, embroiled in their own political revolution, sued for peace, allowing the German Army to fully concentrate its resources on the Western Front, and in a last, desperate throw of the dice they attacked the British and French lines in the spring of 1918. After initial successes, during which the British were almost thrown back to the sea, the last German attempt to win the war petered out. Now the Allies, bolstered by the newly arrived American divisions, went on their own offensive – the last of the ebb.

# 20 – THE BLOOD RED SUN

*Take me home to where the sun never shines.*
*Take me home to be young again*
*Take me home to where I know just what is mine*
*I don't think I can ever feel the sun again*

STEVE ANTIMONY – *Broken Angel*

Since being tainted by the scandal at Wickham Dale Emily Dickens had devoted herself to the service of others. After joining the RAMC she was posted to France where she served as a nurse for almost 18 months, first at battlefield dressing stations near the front line and later at the military hospital in Amiens. Along with her fellow administrating angels, Emily had endured the appalling agonies and suffering of the injured soldiers.

It had been a difficult redemption. Shunned by her family, and tortured by her own feeling of self-doubt and disgust, she was a totally different woman from the moral crusader of the Piccadilly Park Hotel. By the spring of 1918 Emily was close to breaking point. Unable to sleep during her off-duty periods she would lie awake, sometimes comforting herself, occasionally pilfering some morphine to ease her torment. As she tossed and turned, Matron's apposite words came back to haunt her.

*You like to watch, don't you?*

Emily detested the person she had become. Along with some of her colleagues she sought solace in cheap wine and cigarettes. She became close to another nurse, old enough to be her mother, and they drifted into an affair, which only increased her feeling of self-loathing. She had now almost become immune to the suffering of others.

*I bet you like to excite yourself!*

The only decent thing left in her wretched life was the relationship with Will Fulton. She received letters from him spasmodically but, since the Germans had broken through the British lines in March, had heard nothing. Amiens itself was now threatened. If this major road and rail junction fell, the British forces would be cut off from their French allies and the military position desperate.

Emily often wished she were back at the front line. There the soldiers' blood was warmer; the rapid decisions she had to make made the difference between life and death. With the guns close by it was somehow more exciting for her. There were fewer distractions. In Amiens she could walk about the streets in her rest time and forget for a few moments that there was a war going on. But now, with the Germans advancing so rapidly, the position was becoming increasingly hazardous. Here at the hospital, which was based in an old chateau, the injured men often knew their fate, felt their pain more, seemed colder and more resigned to their destiny.

Each day she meticulously studied the casualty lists and hospital admissions, hoping desperately not to see any familiar names, particularly Will's. Having snatched a quick lunch, she would make a daily round of all the wards, checking any new admissions. Then one day in April her heart sank as she saw the name listed on the roster of the surgical ward – Lieutenant Fulton, Royal London Regiment. Forgetting herself, she rushed into the ward and approached the sister, who was sitting at her desk busily writing. 'Sister! Sister! I must speak with you!'

The woman was indeed a sister in two senses, medical and spiritual. Emily knew her as Sister Margaret and that she had a reputation for being a martinet, like many of the Catholic nuns who ran the hospital. The older woman spoke but did not look up. 'Calm yourself, nurse.'

'Please, sister!'

Sister Margaret's expression did not change as she slowly shifted her stern gaze to the pretty young girl sitting across the table. She was a fat, middle-aged woman and wore rimless spectacles on her round, pink face, which was exaggerated by the thick black veil that surrounded it. 'Nurse Dickens, isn't it?'

'Please, Sister, I must speak with you. There is an officer here – Lieutenant Fulton.'

The nun returned to study the papers on her desk. 'What of it?'

'I must see him.' Emily glanced nervously around the huge ward. Some of the patients were groaning in pain, others calling for a nurse or for their mother. 'He's my... my sweetheart!'

'Oh.' The nun's tone was neutral as she studied her notes, her expression grim. Emily sucked her lips nervously, her throat dry. Her fingers fluttered nervously. 'Ah!' said Sister eventually, 'Fulton, just back from the theatre.'

'And?' Emily was almost frantic.

'My child,' replied the nun, her speech quieter, her face softening into a sad smile, 'your friend is in a serious condition.' Emily bit her lip and emitted a little sob. 'He has a piece of shrapnel just below his heart, too dangerous to try and remove. It may move in time and if does, it can be removed. If not, then...' Emily felt the tears welling in her eyes. 'Also,' Sister Margaret added seriously, 'he has a leg wound which has become infected. There is nothing more to be done. We must wait and see.'

'Oh no!' cried Emily. 'May I see him?'

'Very well, I suppose so, but calm yourself, Nurse Dickens. Remember who you are. He's in bed 10.'

'Thank you, Sister.' Emily quickly hurried about the ward, her legs feeling like jelly, until she found the right bed. Taking a deep breath, she pulled up a chair beside it. She bit her tongue sharply, desperately trying to hold back her tears. Will lay still on the bed and was propped up by two pillows. His eyes were closed, and his face was as angelic as ever, but it was pale and pained and his blue eyes were reddened by the suffering. 'Willow,' she murmured, taking his hand, which felt cold and lifeless.

The soldier blinked and slowly opened his eyes. His sad expression briefly brightened. 'Ems is that you?' said a croaky voice.

'I'm here, my darling.'

'Have I died and gone to heaven?' said the weak voice.

Emily forced a pained smile and squeezed the man's hand. 'No, you silly sausage. You are still alive and you're going to be alright.'

Will let his head fall back on the pillow. 'I don't think so, Ems. Fritz has bowled me an unplayable delivery this time.'

Still thinking about his cricket, she thought. 'Nonsense. I'm here now and I'm going to look after you.'

Will closed his eyes, then, after a moment, he spoke again, more weakly. 'Ems?'

Emily moved her head closer to him. 'What is it, my love?'

'I'm so sorry about that night in the hotel. I was a very naughty boy, asking you to...'

'Do you think I care about that now, you daft old date box!' she interrupted, squeezing his hand more tightly. 'Oh, Wills, please don't give up. Are you in much pain?'

'I'm so tired,' he whispered, barely audibly, closing his eyes once more. For a terrible moment, she thought he had gone, but she could still feel his pulse, weak but steady.

'That's it, my poor Willow, you rest now.' Emily could control her feelings no longer, leapt to her feet and ran back along the ward until she came to the door that led out into the grounds. Sister Margaret observed the scene, then frowned and followed the nurse out into the cool afternoon air. Emily stood a few yards from the door, her body heaving with loud sobs, her eyes streaming hot with distress.

'Nurse Dickens!' barked the sister. 'Stop that blubbing immediately! Pull yourself together this instant! Don't you know the first rule of this hospital – no running in the wards!' Emily seemed not to hear, her body bobbing up and down with spasms of lamentation, her hand over her mouth, trying to drown out her own cries. The older woman took the young nurse by the arm. There was a small bench nearby and they sat down together. 'Now, Nurse Dickens,' Sister Margaret began sternly, 'I say again, remember where you are. Remember who you are. We must never let our personal feelings interfere with our responsibilities here.' Her mood softened. 'I know you are not crying for your friend, but for all of them, all those poor broken young men you have seen come and go these past months. We are a special breed, sometimes the final guide between the light and the darkness. You are a good nurse. Emily, isn't it? You are a good nurse, Emily. You are popular with your colleagues and the patients all like you.'

Emily braced herself, looked deeply at the other woman and asked, 'Will he live?'

'Your friend? He is in God's hands now. We can do nothing more.' The sister pulled her arm from Emily's shoulder and fiddled in the pocket of her habit. 'Here, my child, have some of this.' She produced a battered, copper coloured flask and unscrewed the top.

'What is it?' Emily looked a little shocked.

'Brandy. What's the matter, child, even a Bride of Christ can have a small vice, can't she? It's for medicinal purposes only, you understand.'

Sister Margaret smiled as she handed the flask to Emily, who returned a weak smile of her own before taking a big gulp. 'Oh God!' she cried, half choking. 'It's foul!'

'Take some more, slowly. It will fortify you, and don't blaspheme.'

'Sorry, Sister.' Emily took another swig and coughed again, but the bitter liquid warmed her.

'Now, take deep breaths,' ordered the nun. Emily did as she was told, sucking in the cool air, then taking one more swallow of the brandy before handing it back.

'Steady, girl.'

Emily took time to compose herself, the alcohol making her heady. 'I'm sorry, thank you.'

'Better now?'

The younger woman thought deeply for a moment, then said, 'What is God's purpose in allowing this war to continue and prolonging all the misery and suffering?'

Sister Margaret did not care to answer, for it was a question she had asked herself many times. Instead, she said, 'What time are you back on duty?'

'Three o'clock.'

'Then you have time to go to the chapel and pray for your friend. Lift your voice to God. He will hear you.'

Emily regarded the nun and thought how much she reminded her of Olive Blackwell. For a moment it bothered her, then she peered into the woman's eyes and saw a light in them. This woman had a soul. 'God will not hear me, Sister, for I have been an irredeemable sinner.'

*You like to watch, don't you?*

Margaret smiled. 'Goodness! What can a fine child like you have done that God will not forgive? He will surely forgive if you show repentance.'

Emily could not look the woman in the face. 'I cannot speak of it.'

The chubby face looked at her directly. 'You probably think I don't understand, but we are all desperate sometimes. You must take comfort where you can find it.'

Emily stared at the old woman. Did she know? Did she understand? 'I'm really not that kind of woman.'

Margaret smiled again, as if she somehow did understand the girl's anguish. 'Go anyway, child. What harm can it do?'

'I will, Sister. I've never been a religious person, but perhaps...' Her speech trailed away.

'Indeed. Now before you go.' The nun rummaged in her pocket again and brought out a crumpled paper bag, offering the contents to Emily.

'What are they?'

'Peppermints; we don't want your breath smelling on the wards, now do we?' Emily took out one of the stripy sweets and put it in her mouth. 'Now, Nurse Dickens, I must get back to my ward. At 3 o'clock you will go back to yours, calm and composed and behave as you always have done.'

'Yes, Sister, thank you.' Emily smiled to herself as she watched the nun waddle off, wobbling like a fat penguin in her black and white habit. The young nurse then made her way slowly to the rear of the hospital where the little chapel was located. The sun came out, causing her to close her eyes in the glare. For a moment she was back at the school, sitting watching the boys play cricket, or perhaps at the village ground with her father, the father who now ostracised her, along with the rest of her family. She hated her life, hated the person she had become. There was no going back. Then the distant rumble of the guns brought her back to the present. They seemed to be getting closer.

The small chapel was still and gloomy, the only light coming from the doorway and a stained-glass window depicting the crucifixion. There was a middle-aged couple on one side of the aisle, speaking in French to a priest in a white smock. A few other nurses were sitting about in contemplation. Self-conscious and feeling somehow out of place, Emily chose a quiet corner and knelt on the cold stone floor. She put her hands together, feeling a fraud. Initially lost for words, she suddenly found herself whispering, as if some unseen forces were guiding her.

'Oh, dear God, I have committed carnal sins with other women and am beyond redemption. I ask nothing for myself, for I am no longer worthy, but if you could find the grace to spare my poor Willow, I promise to be a good Christian person for what is left of my miserable life. He's a cheeky fellow but a good old stick really.' The words made her gulp and sniffle. The tears came again but she remained in command of herself. 'If you must take him, please don't let him suffer too much.' She paused briefly, then thought of something to add. 'And please put an end to this terrible war and all the misery and anguish it has caused.' Surprised at her own honesty and eloquence, she ended the prayer 'Amen.'

Time passed. Emily knelt as if in a trance, eventually rousing herself to find her fingers entwined in front of her face, so close they were almost touching her nose. She could taste the brandy and peppermint on her hands and lips. In the distance the nearby church bell was tolling the hour; it was time to go back. She stood up, blew her nose and wiped her eyes with a handkerchief, then straightened her crisp uniform. Across the aisle the French woman was sobbing, comforted by the two men at her side – another lost son.

She took a deep breath. 'Time to brisk up and get back to work, Nurse Dickens,' she muttered to herself, then marched purposefully away, feeling a new strength within herself, and returned to being an angel of mercy once more, back to help mend the broken bodies again.

The German offensive eventually ran out of steam and Amiens was saved. The tide of war turned yet again, this time in favour of the Allies, reinforced by several American divisions. Now it was the turn of the Germans to be pushed back – the last of the ebb. The stalemate of the trenches had finally ended, and a war of movement began once again for the first time since 1914. Soon the combatants were back fighting in the valley of the River Marne. The wheel had come full circle.

# 21 – A PULSE IN
# THE INTERNAL MIND

*Our dreams are dripping murder*
*The parted page is turned*
*The race is run, but what have we learned?*

JOHN BIGGLESWORTH – *Providence*

CRAIGLOCKHART SANATORIUM
NR EDINBURGH, SCOTLAND – AUGUST 1918

The war had not gone well for Jack Bigglesworth. In the spring of 1917, he suffered a physical and mental breakdown, brought on by the stress of continuous terror and ceaseless slaughter. He refused to lead his men into battle, claiming nervous exhaustion. At first, he was branded a coward by his senior officers and pushed back into the front line. A few months later he suffered an even more complete breakdown and after several examinations was sent to a new psychiatric hospital in Scotland where most of the patients were suffering from what came to be popularly known as 'shell shock'.

Only the prompt intervention of his regiment's sympathetic medical officer saved Jack from potential court martial and execution for dereliction of duty. He and Kitty Ketteridge had corresponded for over a year but suddenly her letters stopped. Eventually, his mother wrote and told him of how a story had got back to England that he was a coward. She confessed that Kitty had been heartbroken and taken herself off to live in Brighton where, true to her promise, she had become a bus conductress, fallen in with a bad crowd, taken up with a former officer friend of her brother and subsequently got herself pregnant. To hide the disgrace, her family had packed her off to a maiden aunt in Scotland. Not long after, Jack's elderly father died. These events induced his second and more serious breakdown.

It was a sunny summer's afternoon, just like those Jack remembered from his schooldays, when he and his friends would sit on the bank overlooking the Long Field. The sky was blue, the birds were singing, and many flowers were in full bloom. There could be no greater antithesis to the horror and desolation of the Western Front from whence he had come, crushed and broken, a mere shadow of a man. He sat on the bench in the hospital garden and let the sun's rays fall upon his pale skin. He closed his eyes, desperate for some peace and tranquillity from the constant nightmares. He thought of those endless summer days of cricket, competition and good fellowship. He wished he was there again.

After a while a shadow passed in front of the sun and Jack opened his eyes. He blinked and squinted, and recognised the gaunt figure of Doctor Forsyth, the psychiatric specialist who ran the sanitorium. With him were two other men. One he knew as Watkinson, the pugnacious-looking hospital orderly, the other was unknown to him, yet there was something familiar about the man's features. The stranger stood limply, and Watkinson gripped his shoulders to prevent the sad creature from falling.

'Hello, Jack, brought someone to see ye,' said Forsyth in his clipped Edinburgh accent. Jack blinked again but did not comprehend, his slow mind desperately searching for some long-forgotten sliver of memory. 'You were at Wickham School, weren't you, Jack, and you served in the 56th Division in France? Here's an old comrade.'

Jack's mind was a muddle, and he was unable to assimilate what was he was hearing. The newcomer stood perfectly still, gazing into the distance, his face expressionless, but gradually his eyes, grey and lifeless at first, appeared to come alive as he looked towards the soldier on the bench.

'Hello, Biggles.' The voice was faint and unfamiliar, yet he somehow knew the timbre of the man's speech. Suddenly a flash of memory burst into his brain.

'Well, as I live and breathe, Tommy! Tommy Banter, isn't it?' With great care, the orderly manoeuvred the limp body down onto the bench next to Jack until it sat steady, almost motionless, the gaze still distant.

'I'll leave ye two together for a wee while to talk over old times,' said the doctor gaily. 'He may speak to ye, and he may not, but be gentle wi' him.' Forsyth and Watkinson walked off, leaving the two patients sitting on the bench.

'How are you, Tommy?' asked Jack. 'How long have you been here?' The questions were perfunctory, but Tommy did not reply. 'Don't you know me? You do, don't you? We were at school together. I thought they only took officers here.'

He had not seen his old school chum since the fateful day in July 1916 and now hardly recognised him. Gone were the sparkling eyes, the effervescent chatter, the stentorian cackle. In their stead sat a husk of a man, his face thin and almost skeletal, his hair and skin grey, his body emaciated. 'How are your wounds?' Jack was running out of questions. Then he noticed that Tommy was glaring into the distance and that his hands were shaking uncontrollably. A thin trickle of saliva dribbled from his sagging mouth. Jack fell silent, his heart breaking. He didn't know what to say.

At last, the apparition spoke hoarsely, 'Old Tommy Banter's well and truly fucked, that's for sure.' His speech was weedy, almost childlike. Jack stared at his old pal but there was no flicker of acknowledgement. He could feel his eyes welling up. He cried a lot these days, the slightest thing setting him off.

'Oh God, what have they done to you, Tommy?'

'Old Thomas Banter, well and truly fucked this time.'

'Yes, but you are still here, still alive!' The poor creature began to warble to himself in a tinny voice.

*Goodbye Dolly, I must leave you…*

'Did you hear about Freddie?' Jack was crying now.

'Freddie? *I want to go home…*

'Yes, Freddie, remember him? He was your officer.'

'Don't know any Freddie.' *Goodbyee, goodbyee, there's a silver lining in the skyee…*

'Yes, you do, he was your commanding officer. You were his batman. You must remember!' Still there was no sign of recognition. 'He was the captain of our cricket team, the Weston House XI!'

'Batsman?' Tommy turned his face towards Jack and almost broke into a grin. 'Yes, I was a batsman.' The voice was stronger now. 'Freddie and I opened the batting for the House once. He got 50. I got 10.'

*Oh, we don't want to lose you, but we think you ought to go…*

'Yes, yes, that's it, Tommy!' exclaimed Jack, sniffing back the tears.

Tommy stared into his old comrade's face, gawping blankly into his tired eyes. 'I've just shit myself.'

*Though it's hard to leave, I know. I'll… be… tickled to death to go…*

'Oh, Christ, Tommy, so you have,' said Jack, putting his hand to his mouth. 'I'll get a nurse.'

'No, don't do that. Matron'll clear it up.' *Belgium put the kibosh on the Kaiser…* At last, like a candle blown by the wind, Tommy's face seemed to flicker into life.

'You heard about Matron, about what happened at Wickham Dale? My mother wrote and told me all about it.' Jack's speech was almost hysterical.

'Matron?' The candle flickered out again. *The bells of hell go ting-aling-aling…*

'Yes, she got caught in bed with that Emily girl. Kicked her out along with old Stinker. They had been having it off for years. What a turn-up!'

'Off?' *Pack up your troubles in your old kit bag and smile, smile, smile…*

The voice was weaker now, almost trailing away into nothing. A long silence followed, then Tommy spoke once more. His voice was almost a croaky whisper now and his throat gurgled as if he was trying to swallow something. 'Matron was truly kind to me. I cut my knee playing football in the third form. She bandaged it up then took my... my...'

'Took your what, Tommy?'

'Took my... my little todger and rubbed it. She said it would take the pain away. Then she put it in her mouth and I came off.' *While you've a lucifer to light your fag...*

'Did it take the pain away?' Jack was half-laughing and half-crying.

'Yes, Jack, it took the pain away. Can you rub my little todger now, Jack, and make me come off, take the pain away?'

'No, Tommy,' sobbed Jack, tears defeating the laughter, 'I don't think I can do that. Sorry.'

'That's all right. I can do it myself.'

'Not now please, Tommy.'

*What's the use of worrying, it never was worthwhile...?*

To Jack's relief, Doctor Forsyth and Watkinson had returned. The orderly pulled Tommy up from the seat and started leading him away. 'I think he's soiled his pants, Doctor.'

'Don't worry, chum, he's always doing it,' replied the burly nurse. 'Plays with himself a lot as well. Don't worry, sir, I'll see 'im right. You're a naughty boy, aren't you, Tommy? We'll have to change your nappy again.'

*...So, pack up your troubles in your old kit bag and smile... smile... smile*

Jack began to sob helplessly, his chest heaving and a pitiful moaning emanating from the depths of his soul. Forsyth sat down next to the stricken man and put an arm around the other's shoulder. 'I'm sorry, Doctor!' howled Jack.

'Don't apologise, my boy. Tears are a good release for ye.'

After a while, Jack sat up, sniffed and tried to regain some composure. 'Can he recover?'

'Tommy? In time perhaps,' said Forsyth with no emotion. 'In time a man can recover from all the things he has seen and done, but now he is a child again, at least in his mind, which is trying to blot out what has happened since. His mind is like a door, if you like, opening and closing, trying to lock out all the bad memories. He remembers you, but not who you are or where you might have been. Perhaps he only remembers you from before the war. Anything since is buried in his subconscious, but it is there, and he cannot fully erase it, so he shuts everything off, hoping the bad memories will go away. His mind keeps straying off, singing those old marching songs. He is quite an entertainer, isn't he? He cannot be fully cured until he comes to terms with his past. It's the same for you, Jack. How have you been since we last spoke?'

'Ha!' Jack laughed. 'No better. My eyes are always full. My head aches; my guts ache. If I'm not constipated, I've got the runs, never anything in between. I can't sleep; I half-doze and then get these awful flashbacks; they're always the same.'

'Tell me about them. What do you see?'

Jack took a deep breath and braced himself. The thought of the trenches again gave him a sharp pain behind the eyes. 'Alright, I'm running along in no man's land. A shell bursts, awfully close, so loud it totally deafens me. The man running next to me takes the full impact of the explosion, but nothing touches me. One moment he is a man, living, breathing, moving. The next he is no more, nothing more left of him but blood, brains and guts, spraying over me like rain. No trace of a man remains. Nothing. As if he never was. There is a blinding orange light and a terrible, unearthly scream. Then there is nothing at all; deadly quiet. Even the guns have stopped.' Jack gulped, broke down again and wept.

'Is this something that really happened?' asked Forsyth.

'I don't know,' Jack sobbed. 'I… I can't remember.'

'Was this man someone you were close to?'

'I… I… don't know. There was no face. I've never been close to anyone, not at the front anyway.' Something made him think of Kitty. 'There was a girl once.'

'In France?'

'No, in England.'

'What happened to her?'

Jack did not answer for a while, then sighed deeply and said, 'We lost touch. I think she found someone else.'

'Were you in love with her?'

'Love, Doctor Forsyth? I don't think I know what love really is. We were childhood friends, that's all.' Jack lifted his head up, felt the tears running down his hot cheeks.

'Did this contribute to your breakdown?'

Jack did not answer, but then said. 'There is something else. I am in bed, trying to doze. There is this awful smell. I wake up and a dead man is lying next to me, decomposing. I can't get the smell out of my head. I still can't! Then there is another dream. I'm facing a firing squad, and all the Tommies are my old school friends. They fire, but I can feel nothing except... I hear them all laughing...'

There was a long pause. Jack held a hand over his face, sniffling, then asked 'What happened to him?'

'Happened?'

'To Tommy Banter?'

Forsyth shifted his position on the bench and thought for a moment. 'As best as I can recall,' he began, 'Corporal Banter was wounded on the first day of the Somme.'

'Yes, yes, I was there, at Gommecourt,' interrupted Jack excitedly. 'Sorry...'

'He had four shrapnel wounds, painful but not life-threatening. After five months in a hospital, he was pronounced fit for duty again. Then one night he was sent out on a trench raid with an officer and four other men. They were spotted and all killed except Tommy, who was gravely wounded again, though he tried to crawl back to the British lines. He lay in the open for two days and two nights, screaming and moaning, sometimes even laughing, someone said. His battalion could stand it no more and sent out a party to finish him off, for it was driving them all mad...'

'Sounds like Tommy...' Jack started to laugh, then thought better of it.

'But they brought him in, still alive, laughing like a maniac. He was sent to another field hospital, then eventually back to England, then to us, as no one knew what to do with him. His body healed but not his mind.'

'He always was a bit doolally,' smiled Jack. 'Everyone at school used to say so.'

'Well, laddie, he's proper doolally now,' agreed the doctor. 'I'll send him to you again. You may be able to help each other.'

The two men sat in the sunshine for a bit, the Scotsman lighting his pipe and blowing smoke rings into the still air. 'You must leave here soon, Jack,' he murmured thoughtfully.

'I know,' said his companion. 'They won't send me back, will they? I couldn't bear it. I'd rather die.' Jack could feel himself shaking.

'No, no, laddie,' said the doctor soothingly. 'You needn't worry yourself on that score. The war will be over soon anyway. I heard the Germans are retreating all along the line now. They won't let their own country be invaded. They will sue for peace. Their people are starving, so they say.'

'When I was home on leave everyone seemed to think it was a game out there, like some giant cricket match between us and the enemy, like we were playing Australia in the Ashes. No one had the faintest idea what was going on. Do you know, I walked down the street once in my civvies and this pretty girl came up to me and gave me a white feather and said I should be ashamed...' He started to break down again.

'I know, laddie.'

'They have no conception, Doctor Forsyth, especially the women, the fat profiteers and the politicians who want to prolong the war for their own ends, so they can sell more guns, more uniforms and supplies to the armies. They are making a fortune out of our suffering. We could have had a peace settlement in 1916...'

'I know, Jack.'

'I wrote to the newspapers,' Jack became excited. 'I told them the truth...'

'I know you did. I read your letter. We must censor all mail from here. I didn't send it.'

'But why?'

'The time is not right yet for people to know the truth. All they want is an end to the war. The time will come when you, and the likes of you, can tell your story, but the country is not ready to hear it now. You are a very literate man, Jack. I read some of your poems. After the war you must get them published. They may be ready to listen then, but not now, not yet.'

'Not now, not yet,' Jack repeated with a sigh. 'I'm tired, Doctor. I'm so tired' I lie on my bed at night and try to sleep. I want to go to sleep and never wake up again, but I can't sleep – that same vision, just before the dawn.'

'Your time will come. You are stronger than you think, believe me.'

The sun was slowly going down. Jack suddenly felt hungry. He usually ate little but felt the need for something now. The two men stood up and slowly walked back to the main hospital building, passing some of the inmates sitting in wheelchairs, sad wrecks that once were men; men who went out to battle grim and glad, but now children, with eyes that hate you, broken and mad.

# 22 – AN UNEXPECTED VISITOR

*Summer's last ball; bowled, batted and run,*
*Scored and recorded, and now there are none.*

JOHN BIGGLESWORTH – *The Last Ball*

One rainy day in the early autumn of 1918, Professor Jeremy Brooman was sitting alone in his headmaster's study at Wickham Dale College. A new term had just begun. The news from France was encouraging at last, and the allied forces were advancing on all fronts.

He still had many problems, however: the school was nowhere near full complement, its reputation still suffering from the recent scandals. The head's mood was sombre. So many boys he had taught in the past few years were now dead, fallen in sacrifice for king and country. Such a useless waste of life, he often reflected. When he thought of some of the boys who had passed through his care in recent times, so full of life, ambition and expectation, he fell into a hopeless slough of despond.

His meditations were interrupted by a knock on the door. 'Enter!' he barked, almost absent-mindedly. A young first-year boy, whom he did not know, meekly opened the door and spoke.

'Excuse me, sir, sorry to bother you, but there's a gentleman here to see you.'

'A gentleman?'

'Pardon, sir, a British officer.'

'What? Make up your mind, boy. Well, send him in.'

The boy scuttled away and a portly fellow in the full-dress uniform of a staff officer entered. At first Brooman did not recognise him. Then realisation dawned. 'Good gracious, Mister Hill, isn't it? Please come in, my boy. How are you?'

Billy Hill moved smartly to the head's desk and offered his hand across the table. 'It's Captain Hill now, sir.'

'Of course, it is. Please sit down, my boy. It is good to see you again. I hardly recognised you with your fine whiskers. I see, however, that your shadow has not grown less in the past four years.'

'No, sir,' agreed Billy, looking at his increasing paunch as he sat down in the chair opposite.

'Never mind, young fellow, at least you are still alive.'

'Yes, sir, I haven't had such a bad time of it really. I was on Allenby's staff for a while. Then, when he was posted to the Middle East, I applied for a position at GHQ with Field Marshal Haig.'

'Ah, Haig, mmm.'

'Yes, sir, I know what people think back here, that he's a butcher, serving up the boys as endless cannon fodder. But he's quite a decent chap, really.'

'Is he now?' replied Brooman evenly. 'Well, I'll have to take your word for it.'

'I've got a nice little billet for myself in Montreuil; plenty of good food.'

'Very nice for you, Captain Hill, or may I call you William?'

'Of course, sir. I must say, I do feel a bit guilty sometimes, with the chaps in the trenches having such a miserable time of it.'

'Indeed. Have you seen any action?'

'Not until the German offensive in the spring. I was sent up the line and ended up taking over a battalion that had lost all its officers. It was hairy for a while. I've never been so scared in my life! I don't know how I got through it.'

'Obviously, you did. So, what else have you been up to?' Brooman's tone, as always, seemed slightly terse to Billy.

'Mainly liaison stuff with the Frogs. I knew my languages would come in handy one day. Spot of interrogation with German prisoners, mainly officers, that kind of thing.'

'Well,' sighed the head, 'we all have our part to play.'

'Yes, sir. Have you heard any news of other chaps; the old cricket team from 1914?'

Brooman looked through the window, out into the distance. 'William, there are few of you left now. Many of them have paid the ultimate price.'

'Yes, sir, I heard. Freddie… Have you heard anything of Jack Bigglesworth?'

The head did not answer but said instead, 'There have been many changes here, as you can see.'

'Yes,' agreed Billy, glad for the sudden change of subject. 'I heard about Professor Hughes, Matron and…'

'Professor Purviss,' Brooman concluded. Billy looked down to the floor. 'You must not reproach yourself, my boy. He was a very wicked man who prayed on the innocent. He has been punished for his sins.'

'Yes, sir, I understand.'

'You know, William, I was not unaware of the malfeasance that might have occurred before the war, but without any proof I was powerless.'

'It's all right, sir, I understand. What's done is done.'

'Indeed. Anyway, the school is slowly getting back on its feet. Times are hard, but the college will recover in due course, just as our country will.'

Outside, the rain had stopped, and a watery sun was struggling through the grey clouds. For a short time neither man felt like speaking any more, then Brooman said, 'The war is going well now, William.'

'Yes, sir, our last offensive knocked the stuffing right out of old Fritz, hit him properly for six. They're on the run for good this time.'

'Indeed, they are, my boy. Indeed, they are. Before their own territory is invaded, they will call for an armistice. Everyone has suffered enough.' He paused before adding, 'And to what purpose?' Billy nodded.

'Tell me, my lad, what will you do once the war is over?'

'Go back to my father's business, sir. I'm sorry to say he has done rather well out of this war.'

'As many have, sadly. That is the way of things, William, but I wish you success in all your endeavours. You were a bright boy, if a little too easily distracted. You will come back and see us from time to time, won't you? Until then, you must take care of yourself.'

'Of course, sir,' said Billy brightly, then his smile vanished suddenly.

'What is it, my boy?'

'I was going to say that... I look forward to the... the pupil reunions.' His voice tailed away to nothing as he remembered. 'It was only a few years ago that...' It was no use. He could not go on. The memories were too sad.

'We have lost many friends, William,' Brooman's speech was equally cheerless. He took a deep breath. 'There are times... when... it is almost... unbearable.'

\*

The German Army was pushed further and further back on the Western Front. Even the 'Hindenburg Line' – a complex defence system believed to be almost impregnable – was breached by the Allies in the autumn of 1918. With their forces on the point of giving up, the Germans had no option but to sue for peace. Finally, on the 11th hour of the 11th day of the 11th month of 1918, in the fifth year of the war, the guns finally fell silent. What started as a minor squabble in eastern Europe had escalated into the greatest global conflict ever known, surpassing even the Napoleonic wars of the previous century. Although many figures could not be accurately confirmed, an estimated 10 million soldiers had perished during the four-and-a-quarter years of fighting. Millions more were irreparably damaged, both physically and psychologically, by their experiences. The slaughter among the warring nations was unprecedented: Russia lost nearly two million men, Germany over a million-and-a-half, the French not many fewer and the Austro-Hungarian Empire almost one million.

Britain suffered almost as badly, with nearly 700,000 of their service personnel dying and over two million wounded. Conscription had been introduced in 1916 when the flood of volunteers fell to a trickle, and in all, more than eight million Britons – one sixth of the population – passed through the armed services during the conflict. The average strength of the British Army between 1914 and 1918 was more than three million. The Great War, as it came to be known, was the first truly mechanised war between nations, and saw the introduction of new and terrifying weapons of destruction – tanks, poison gas, flame-throwers, submarines, huge guns that could thunder forth projectiles for miles, and aeroplanes that could rain down destruction on innocent civilian populations. The fall of eagles was unprecedented: the Russian tsar and all his family were massacred; the German Hohenzollern dynasty fell, and with that country on the verge of revolution, the seeds of a second war were already being sown; the feeble Austro-Hungarian Empire – which had started the whole conflagration back in 1914 – also crumbled, as did the Turkish Ottoman Empire. The map of Europe was re-written, with princes and politicians the world over in total accord that such a disaster should never be allowed to befall the civilised world again.

The Wickham Dale Cricket XI resumed its fixtures in 1919. In the pavilion, a board was erected listing the team's former members who had fallen in defence of freedom, never to raise a bat again.

*

Seven summers passed. By then, the country had changed forever since the end of the war and the liberal England of

Asquith and Lloyd-George had died a strange death. The 1918 Representation of the People Act enfranchised men over 21 and women over 30. In 1919 the victorious Allies met at Versailles to rewrite the map of Europe. A worldwide peace organisation – The League of Nations – was founded, primarily to prevent a repeat of the global cataclysm that had just ended. Ireland, long a thorn in Britain's side, was granted independence, partially at least. The Allies Reparation Commission levied war compensation of £6.5 billion to Germany, a nation already on its knees. She would never pay it, her national humiliation rendering a further conflict almost inevitable. In 1924 Britain's first Labour government was elected.

# 23 – THE LAUGHING HEART'S PEACE

*Saints upon white horses, demand appreciation,*
*While jokers in funny hats try to appease the nation*

STEVE ANTIMONY – *Nemesis and Nostalgia*

BRIGHTON, ENGLAND – 1924

England went about its usual business, but the peace hung heavier than the war had ever done. Sports like football and cricket were as popular as ever and the working classes still spent their summer holidays by the sea. It was a rainy day in September and Brighton's Palace Pier was doing slow business, as was the End of The Pier Summer Review. The show went on three times a day and featured minor music hall artists of the time, including one Tommy 'Chuckles' Banter – 'A laugh a minute or your money back!'

Tommy had led a nomadic life since being discharged from the Craiglockhart Clinic in 1919, seemingly cured, and was determined to forge some sort of career in show business. Various music hall, variety hall and repertory companies later he found himself opening the bill on Brighton Pier on a cold, wet Monday afternoon. The theatre was sparsely populated, and the mood was a little listless.

'Now then, now then!' enthused Tommy, who, as bottom of the bill, was first up on the stage, nothing more than a warm-up act. 'It's all 'appenin' missus! It's all 'appenin'! Now then, this smart old geezer goes into a respectable club down the West End, dressed up to the nines, accompanied by a tarty lady, young enough to be his daughter. Wait for it! So, he says to the barman, "Whisky and soda please, and a gin and tonic for the lady", to which the bartender replies, "The lady looks a bit young, sir. Is she an adult?", and the girl pipes up an' comes back with, "No, I'm an adulteress!". Ha, ha, I said it was all 'appenin'! A laugh a minute or your money back!'

There was little response from the audience apart from a mild murmur. Tommy's routine was saucy but never blue. Undaunted, he carried on. 'The same man walked into another bar and said "Owww!" It was an iron bar! I said it was all 'appenin' missus, ha, ha, ha!' Still no response, so Tommy tried again. 'I say, I say, I say, what d'you call an Italian with a rubber toe? Roberto!' More groans from the sparse attendance.

A group of hobbledehoys had congregated near the back of the auditorium, fuelled by a few lunchtime ales. 'When are you gonna tell some funny jokes!' one of them bellowed. Tommy was not amused that their barracking got a bigger laugh than his efforts but ignored the heckling and continued, 'A man goes to see one of them, whatsitnames, trick-cyclists – You know what I mean, missus? – and says "Doctor, sometimes I think I'm a marquee and sometimes I think I think I'm a wigwam", and the Doc replies, "I know what's wrong with you son, you're too tense!" Geddit, missus? Two tents! It's all 'appenin'!'

'Get off! Yelled one of the louts.

'Bring on the dancing bears!' shouted another.

Tommy soldiered on as best he could, moving on to a little dance routine that caused his war injuries to pain him and finishing with his usual song. The band sparked up in a perfunctory manner and off he went:

*Private Perks is a funny little codger, with a smile, a funny smile...*

*... Five feet none, he's an artful little dodger, with a smile, a funny smile...*

*... Flush or broke, he'll 'ave 'is little joke... He can't be suppressed...*

*... All the other fellows 'ave to grin... when he gets this off 'is chest...*

Tommy waved his hands and shouted 'Hi!'

*... All together now...*

'Piss off!'

*... Pack up your troubles in your ol' kit bag and smile, smile, smile...*

*... While you've a lucifer to light your fag, smile boys, that's the style...*

'Get off, you boring git, the war's over!'

*... What's the use of worrying. It never was worthwhile...*

*... So, pack up your troubles in your old kit bag and smile, smile, smile...*

'Boooo!'

Tommy ignored the hecklers and waved himself off. 'You've been a fantastic audience. It's been a laugh a minute. See you all again an' enjoy your 'oliday. This is Tommy 'Chuckles' Banter signing off until next time.'

'Thank gawd for that!'

'Give us our money back then!'

'Fuckin' morons!' complained Tommy as he passed the next act – a troupe of French jugglers – and stormed into the communal dressing room backstage.

'What's the matter then, my little tickling stick, act not going down well today?' Connie Crabtree was the resident singer. A failed diva, she was a gin-soaked cockney dame in her mid-thirties, grotesquely fat and a chanteuse of bawdy songs and sentimental lullabies.

'Don't know why I fuckin' bother!' moaned Tommy, rummaging through the drawer of his dressing table.

'You should've got yer cock out, Tom. That always gets a laugh!' It was Julie, one of the cheeky teenage chorus girls from across the room. Hoots of laughter followed.

'Very amusing,' said Tommy dryly. 'Ere, who's been at me gin again?'

'Sorry, dux,' apologised Connie, 'I was feelin' a bit thirsty earlier. If you weren't such a stingy bastard an' gone an' marked the bottle, no one would've noticed.'

'Bloody cheek!'

'Never mind, darlin', ol' Connie'll make it up to you. Come 'ome with me tonight and we'll 'ave a good time.' She put her flabby arms around Tommy's scrawny neck and squeezed. 'You can show us your war wounds if y'like.'

'Do me a favour, Con, I might be 'ungry but I ain't starvin'.'

'You cheeky bleeder!'

'I wouldn't if I were you, Thomas my old son,' said Ted Thorpe, the vulgar ventriloquist sitting at the next table. 'The last geezer to give Connie a poke disappeared up her charlie and hasn't been seen since!'

'An' 'ow would you know?' returned Connie. 'You'd need a bleedin' microscope to find your todger. Wouldn't even touch the sides!'

'Gawd! everyone's a bleedin' comedian 'ere!' observed Tommy.

'Everyone except you!' cried another voice from the chorus line. That got a bigger laugh than anything all day.

After that, the room settled down. Then Connie remembered something. 'There was a bloke looking for you earlier.'

'Bloke? What bloke?' Tommy seemed a trifle nervous.

'Dunno, didn't give 'is name. Posh looking cove in a smart suit. 'Ad a whiff o' lavender about 'im if you ask me.'

'What, you mean one of them?' joked Ted, flapping a limp hand.'

'Not your fancy man is 'e, Tommy?' giggled Julie the chorus girl.

'Fuck off!'

'Blimey! Our Tommy don't take the tube up the chocolate factory, does 'e?' bawled Annie May, another busty bird from the chorus, sparking more howls of laughter.

'Our Tommy's as straight as a donkey's dick,' confirmed Connie. 'You went to a public school, didn't you, my darlin'?'

'Did 'e say anything?' asked Tommy, still frowning.

'As a matter o' fact 'e did,' Connie recalled. 'Said 'e was gonna watch your turn, then 'e'd be outside the stage door at two.'

Tommy cleaned off his stage make-up and, instead of leaving by the artistes' door, exited through the main body of the theatre, creeping along to the side entrance and peeping around the corner to see if he could spot the man. It was drizzling very slightly and the sea below was choppy and uninviting. Opposite the side exit a smartly dressed man was leaning over the balustrades, smoking a cigar and gazing out to sea. As if sensing Tommy's presence he turned and spotted him. Tommy was about to hop back round the corner when the man called out, 'Mister Banter!'

Just then a young boy ran up with a small book and pencil in his hands. 'Can I have your autograph please, Mister Chuckles?'

'No, fuck off, kid!' The boy ran bawling back to his parents, who gave Tommy a look of utter disgust and walked off. Tommy took no notice and instead concentrated on the man in the smart suit. Somewhat reluctantly he emerged from the shadows. The man did not look like a bookmaker or a copper, but he did look a bit 'queer'. 'Do I know you, squire?'

'Not yet, Mister Banter, but hoping. My card.' The man's speech was cultured but not quite that of a toff. Tommy put on his spectacles and squinted at the small writing:

*Maurice Bellman – Theatrical Agent, 25 Victoria Square, Brighton-on-Sea*

'Sorry, pal,' said Tommy, 'I've already got an agent.'

'Quite so, Mister Banter. Quite so. Shall we walk for a while.'

''Ere, what's your game!' Tommy took a step back.

'Please, Mister Banter,' the man spread his arms wide, 'No game, nothing to worry about, I assure you.'

'So, what d'you want then?'

'I caught your act today, Tommy. I can call you Tommy, can't I? Very jocular. Very comical.'

'Get to the point.'

'Very well,' Bellman stopped and doffed his hat theatrically. 'Thomas, how would like to be a film star?'

'Come again?'

'A film star, Thomas my boy. I can make you famous.'

Tommy stopped and stared at the man. He was younger than he had first thought and quite distinguished in a handsome way. 'What are you on about? Do I look like Charlie Chaplin?'

The man raised his hands in the air and wiggled them back and forth. 'Erm… in a way you have banged the proverbial nail on its head already, so to speak.'

'I'll bang you on the 'ead if you don't tell me what this is all about!'

'Don't be so hasty, my boy. Please let me explain. I represent British Lion Moving Pictures. We are making a series of cinematic comedies and we're looking for a comic character. Just a small part, you understand, but... erm... quite rewarding.'

'How rewarding?' Tommy was getting interested now.

'Shall we say £10 a film for about two weeks' work, then if the producers like you...'

'Silent films?'

'Absolutely.'

'So, I don't get to tell any jokes?'

The man made another wide gesture. 'Tommy, it's the look we're after. You look funny. You're a clown and you have, shall we say, minor celebrity status, and to be frank, my boy, judging by your performance today, silent films is a better option for you.'

'You cheeky bastard!'

'Come on, Tommy old son, you look funny. People laugh at your character, not at your jokes. What do you say? Think it over.'

'I look funny,' echoed Tommy. 'I bleedin' well look funny!'

Bellman put his hat back on his head, stared out to sea, thought for a minute then turned back to Tommy. A breeze was getting up and both men were starting to feel the cold. 'Tommy,' he began again in a more conciliatory tone, 'do you really want to spend the rest of your career in fleapits like this, in front of rows of empty seats? You have potential, my boy. Potential. Soon there will be talking pictures. Think of the potential in that.'

'Potential, is that what I've got?' thought Tommy out loud. The chill was beginning to get to his old wounds, which were still stiff after all these years. The man was right. What was the future in a place like this? What did he have to lose? He put Bellman's card in his pocket. 'I'll be in touch.'

A couple of old biddies, huddled up against the rain and cold, were sitting on a bench nearby and staring at the two men. Tommy stared back at them, and they averted their gaze. Then he started to hum to himself:

*Pack up your troubles in your old kit bag…*

# 24 – A PEACE UNSHAKEN

*They – shall not sleep. They – shall not rest.*
*In love and war, they were the best.*
*Ne'er found wanting in the greatest test,*
*their hearts of oak and wonder.*
*They – once so brave and tall and straight,*
*oblivious to their tortured fate.*
*Lie twisted, broken, with eyes of hate,*
*their future torn asunder,*
*They – children of their earthly shroud,*
*danced singing madly through the crowd.*
*Mothers, fathers, justly proud,*
*reward the nation's blunder.*

JOHN BIGGLESWORTH – *They*

When the war ended, and following his release from the army, Jack Bigglesworth had retired to the outskirts of a little village in Sussex, rented a simple cottage and lived a solitary existence, bar a few animals he kept, and wrote his first book – a thin tract of poetry entitled *They Shall Not Sleep* which was published in 1921 by a small firm in London. But war poets were ten a penny and only 500 copies were ever printed. Fewer were sold, but nevertheless, Jack earned enough to start work on a much greater project, provisionally titled *Ever England,* a novel based around his experiences in the war. He augmented this sparse income by growing vegetables and selling them in the local market, which was his only real contact with the outside world. For five years he endured an unvarnished life, content, in a modest way, though perhaps never genuinely happy. He was trying to forget his past, without having any conception of a future.

It was a cool day in late September and as usual Jack was pottering about in his vegetable garden, lifting the last fruits of his labours to sell in the market, hoping to make enough to buy a decent meal and maybe a small bottle of whisky. So engrossed was he in his work that he failed to notice a small boy walking up the garden path. His exertions had made him sweat slightly, despite the cool temperature, but his blood seemed to inexplicably run cold as he became aware of the child standing before him.

The late afternoon sun was in Jack's eyes as the boy spoke. 'Good afternoon, sir.' His speech was polite and precise. 'My mother asked me to introduce myself to you. My name is John. How do you do.'

The address sounded rehearsed. Jack smiled weakly at the boy, getting to his feet and wiping a dirty hand on his trousers before gently touching the hand that young John had offered. The child must have been about seven or eight years old. His clothes – a grey coat and cap to match – were slightly shabby but his hands and face were clean. It was not until he felt the lad's relaxed grip and gazed into the innocent face that a strange feeling ran through him, a curious shiver that deeply disturbed his tranquillity. The boy was not from the village, that much was certain. His eyes were light brown and the mop of hair under the school cap was fair without being yellow.

Stiffly, Jack stood to his full height and looked down upon his little visitor. 'How do you do, John. That's my name, though most people call me Jack.' A thought followed. 'And where is your mother?' The boy motioned towards the garden gate where a young woman stood, expressionless. She was dressed in a pale brown coat and bonnet and wearing a pair of old-fashioned rimless spectacles. Her figure was fuller than Jack remembered but he knew her instantly.

'Hello, Johnny.'

Jack's heart missed a beat, several in fact. He could only stare, tongue-tied. Freddie, his Old English Sheepdog, broke the spell, a flurry of fur and canine excitement as, stick in mouth, he bounded up to a possible new playmate. The dog dropped the stick at the boy's feet, then sat down and yipped. Distracted by this, Jack did not notice Kitty walk through the gate.

'Can I play with him, Mother?' asked the boy expectantly. Kitty looked at Jack, silently questioning.

'Throw the stick,' said Jack nervously. The boy did as he was bid. Freddie bounced up and down a couple of times and ran off barking with joy, little John in pursuit.

'Will he be alright?' Kitty's voice sounded tired, even world weary.

'Of course, Freddie's a harmless old thing.' Jack studied her more closely. Her face seemed rounder, and her hair was longer. She appeared plainer than ever, not the sort of woman anyone would notice in a crowd.

Kitty did not return his gaze, but sighed and asked,' Can we go inside? My feet are killing me. I'd die for a cup of tea.'

'Y... yes... yes, of course.' Jack was all a dither, his heart thumping and head spinning, as he pushed open the wooden front door and ushered her inside. 'I... I'm sorry, the place is a bit of a mess. Come into the kitchen. I'll put the kettle on.'

'You look thin,' Kitty said, 'but I like your beard.'

She sat down exhaustedly in a chair by the kitchen table as Jack filled the kettle, his mind a turmoil of questions. Finally, one pushed its way to the front of his mind. 'How on earth did you find me?'

'It's a long story,' Kitty sighed. 'Johnny, the kettle's full.' The water was overflowing into the sink and splashing Jack. 'Same old Johnny,' she laughed weakly, 'all fingers and thumbs.'

*Johnny*, he thought. What was she doing here? How did she find me? No one had called him that for a long time; he hadn't spoken to his mother for years. He nervously lit the gas on the stove with a match, aware that Kitty was watching his every move. An uneasy silence followed as he busied himself cleaning a pair of cups, before the words tumbled out. 'I'm sorry, Kitty, I let them all down.'

'What are you talking about?' she asked wearily.

Jack could feel his eyes welling up. 'I couldn't go on. My nerves were shattered. I just couldn't take any more. I had a complete breakdown. My mother told me... about you... and...'

'And what, Johnny? What lies did she tell you?' Kitty's voice was stern but neutral, betraying no emotion. 'She never liked me. Now she hates me. Our mothers were best friends since schooldays. They haven't spoken to each other for years.'

'She doesn't hate you, Kitty.' Jack stood up and walked to the kitchen window, watching the boy and his dog frolicking happily in the garden. 'She told me a story had got back to England that… that I was a coward, and you were… ashamed and… heartbroken…'

Kitty interrupted excitedly. 'I would never be ashamed of you, Johnny, whatever you may have done! I could never be… sorry… go on.'

'She said you had run away to Brighton, fallen in with a bad crowd and…'

'And what?'

'Got yourself …' He couldn't bring himself to speak the words.

'Into trouble? Johnny, come and sit down, please.' Jack did as he was told. 'I never went to Brighton. When they found out I was pregnant my parents sent me away to live with my maiden aunt in Edinburgh, to hide their embarrassment. My father wanted to kill you. We had a massive fight, and I said the Germans would do it instead, or something silly like that. I haven't spoken to him since. He tore up any letters you sent, and I couldn't find out what had happened to you. Auntie May said you might have been lost, but I didn't believe anything anyone told me. I knew you were still alive.'

The kettle whistled but Jack ignored it and went to stand by the window again. Kitty had regained some composure. 'I'll be mother then, shall I?' She switched off the gas and moved silently to where Jack was watching the boy playing. Her hand gently touched his arm and the intimacy awakened old feelings he thought had long since died.

She sighed deeply and murmured softly, 'You knew, didn't you, the moment you saw him?' Jack closed his eyes. 'Oh, Johnny, he's so much like you.' She squeezed his arm. 'Quiet, studious and solitary, but bright as a button. He's top of the class in nearly every subject at school. My aunt was a headmistress and she got me a job as a teacher.'

Jack stared at the boy, and could neither speak nor take it all in. Tears welled in his eyes. Kitty pulled him away from the window and he sat down as she made the tea.

'Johnny, please listen to me. There's something else I need to tell you.' Kitty looked very earnest. 'I also lied to you.'

'Lied?'

'Yes, Johnny, that night in the hotel, when I said it would be safe to make love to me. I knew it wasn't. I knew it was my time.'

'Sorry... lied... time... I don't understand.'

'Oh, Johnny, you are such a dimwit sometimes, like a light bulb flickering on and off! I had some silly notion I would never see you again and... well... silly, wilful impetuous old Kitty, never stopping to think of the consequences...' She hesitated and smiled, disarming him as she had when they were little.

'I don't remember much about that night,' Jack recalled. 'I was very drunk.' Little Johnny ran past the window, followed by Freddie who was barking loudly. The boy waved and ran on, kicking a battered football.

Kitty put her hand on Jack's and gazed into his sad face. He thought she looked like a schoolmarm. As if sensing this, Kitty took off her spectacles and put them on the table. Jack could not help but notice that her eyes which, once so sparkling and mischievous, now appeared dull and defeated.

A sliver of memory filtered into Jack's head, sparked by the closeness of her body. Her flesh, soft and cool; her fragrance, overwhelming his fuddled senses; her frustration, as they fumbled drunkenly in the dark. Did that really happen? Did she really say, 'I've longed for this moment. There's only ever been you, Johnny?'

Kitty rambled on in her old style. 'Auntie May passed me off as a war widow. Look, I'm still wearing that silly ring!' She wiggled it on her hand and giggled, just as she had that night in the hotel. 'I'm not sure everyone believed it. There was a teacher at the school who was truly kind to me, but he was old enough to be my father. He even asked me to marry him, to make an honest woman of me. Ha! Imagine that! Kitty an honest woman!'

'Why didn't you marry him? Wouldn't it have solved all your problems?'

Kitty let out another deep sigh and shrugged. 'I didn't love him.'

'Did that matter?'

'Of course it mattered!' Kitty sipped her tea, then asked, 'Johnny, do you have a woman?' It seemed a familiar question.

'No'

'I thought not, judging by the state of this place.'

Jack didn't respond, but asked instead, 'So how *did* you find me?'

'Like I said, after Johnny was born, I got a job at the school. My auntie was a kindly old soul. She never married or had any children of her own. One day she gave me a copy of your book. I don't know where she got it. That's how I knew you were still alive, that somehow you had survived. I don't know where she found it. Perhaps your mother sent it. Poor Auntie May died a few weeks ago, but before she did, she told me the truth, so I was set on burning my bridges and trying to find you. Your mother wouldn't see me. She wouldn't even acknowledge her own grandson! I know I brought shame on both our families, but it made me so angry! So, I went to see your publisher.'

'What, old Hemingway?'

'Yes, funny old codger, isn't he? At first, he wouldn't give me your address, but I badgered and badgered him until he told me where to find you. I think he felt sorry for me. You know your Kitty; like a dog with a bone.'

Jack wasn't sure whether he did know his Kitty anymore. He was beginning to feel some resentment, her turning up out of the blue as if nothing had happened, with a child in tow that she claimed was his, disturbing his long sought-for tranquillity. He may have these thoughts, but he could never express them. There was another silence as they sipped their tea. He turned and watched the boy exploring the garden, Freddie following him faithfully.

'Does he know who I am?' Jack asked at length.

Kitty gave a look of surprise, as if it were one of his silly questions. 'Of course, he does! He knows everything. He even read your poems. Some of them he can recite off by heart, though he doesn't understand quite all of it. I told you he was bright. I told him you had been terribly injured in the war and had to go far away for a long time to get better, and that one day we would all be together. Drink your tea, Johnny, it's getting cold.'

Another awkward silence followed, neither of them knowing what to say next. Then Jack thought of something. 'So, you got the vote then?'

'Rubbish!' Kitty's reaction startled him. 'Not for another two years, thank you very much! How is it that a man can have a vote at 21 but a simple woman has to wait another nine years; the usual muddled compromise!'

Jack offered a weak smile. 'Same old Kitty, always angry at something.'

'There's always something to be angry about!' She saw he was teasing, and her frown eased to an embarrassed smile. 'Kitty on her soapbox again.'

The exchange eased the tension. 'What will you do?' Jack asked, knowing it was a leading question.

Kitty gave him another of her disapproving looks, tilting her head the way she always did as a child. 'Do? What can I do? I am an unmarried woman with an illegitimate child. I have no money. What future can there be for someone like me? I see the way people look at me, whispering behind my back. I can feel it in a glance or hear it in a word.'

Jack said nothing as Kitty sighed again. She looked almost close to tears. 'Johnny, I had to come. I had to find you. You must surely understand that. There's no one left any more. I can't go home again. The shame is too much for my family. Oh, Johnny, please don't send me away! I couldn't bear it! I'm so sorry for everything. Can you ever forgive me?'

She started to cry and took a small handkerchief from her purse to dab her eyes. Jack remembered something from their childhood. She never cried, even when she once fell out of a tree and cut her knee open. She never cried. 'Please don't send me away!'

Jack stood up again and walked to the window, though he could no longer see the boy and his dog. Kitty composed herself and came and stood beside him. She took his hands. There was sadness in her eyes. 'Oh, Johnny, there hasn't been a day when I haven't thought of you. Little Johnny has been such a joy to me, the only good thing in my miserable life. I've paid for my wickedness a thousand times.'

'Kitty, I was in a psychiatric hospital for six months.' Jack's voice was trembling. 'They call it shell shock. I couldn't do anything for myself... I... I.'

'Oh, my poor darling. Are you better now?'

'Better? It never leaves me. I still have nightmares, flashbacks. It never goes away.' She put her arms around Jack's neck and kissed him softly on his cheek.

'You won't send me away, will you? There's no one left now. The war has taken everything. I was so afraid you wouldn't want to see me. That's why I didn't write to you first.'

What could he say? He hadn't seen her for more than eight years, and here she was again, turning up like a bad penny, picking holes in everything he did and trying to run his life. An hour ago, he had been almost content though still empty inside, although in truth he had grown weary of his hermit-like existence.

She pulled away from him slightly. 'Johnny, remember when we were little children, the day we swore to become blood brothers, or brothers and sisters, whatever? We cut our hands and let our blood run together, swearing we'd always be friends and take care of each other.'

'We're not children anymore, Kitty.'

'No, we're not. We're all grown up now and no one can tell us what to do or keep us apart. I was always getting you into trouble, wasn't I? There is only you and I left now. I think there only ever was you and me.'

'I never understood why you liked me.'

'Oh, Johnny, you old silly!' She looked deeply into his troubled eyes. 'You know I was never happy as a child. My parents wanted another boy and I turned up. I was a difficult birth, and after me, my mother couldn't have any more children. Julian was always their favourite. I was only really happy playing with you. You let me scold you and tease you and bully you, and never complained. You were such a lamb. You let silly, spoiled old Kitty be herself and I loved you for that, even before I knew what it meant.'

She moved her hands to cradle his face. She seemed taller than Jack remembered, almost as tall as him, so when she nuzzled his cheek their tears mingled, just as their blood had once done. 'I have always loved you, Johnny. I always will.'

Just then the boy came running in but stopped dead when he saw his parents embracing. Kitty held out her hand and the child ran to his mother, hugging her legs. Freddie followed him in, the battered old football hanging from his mouth. Dropping it on the stone floor, the dog sat down on its back legs and barked loudly, demanding attention.

'Be quiet, you silly mutt!' ordered his new mistress. The dog sank down on all fours, rested his head on his front paws and whimpered.

Jack knew then that his world would never be the same again.

# EPILOGUE
# AND WE WERE YOUNG

*With proud thanksgiving, a mother for her children,*
*England mourns for her dead across the sea.*
*Flesh of her flesh they were, spirit of her spirit*
*Fallen in the cause of the free.*

LAURENCE BINYON – *For the Fallen*

So, what became of them, those who were young and went to battle, straight of limb, true of eye, steady and aglow, the sons of 1914, the cricketers of Wickham Dale?

John Alfred Walter 'Jack' Bigglesworth, Second Lieutenant, 7th Battalion, Middlesex Regiment, was no celebrated war hero, unlike his illustrious distant cousin James, of the Royal Flying Corps. He married Kitty, who bore him two further children, both girls, and eventually their families were reconciled. His *Ever England* novel was a critical and financial success, despite being initially panned as unpatriotic, and he subsequently enjoyed a flourishing career as a novelist and historian.

Kitty became the headmistress of the village school and a respected local councillor, despite her views often being regarded as radical. She campaigned determinedly for women's rights. Like his father, John Bigglesworth Junior turned out to be a fine cricketer and had an unsuccessful trial for Sussex. He persuaded his father to come out of retirement and join him in the village team at the age of 38. Jack was still playing just weeks before his death 40 years later. Kitty passed away less than a month after, dying of a broken heart.

Thomas Edward Banter, Corporal, 10th Battalion (Sportsmen's) Royal London Regiment, found brief fame as Tommy Tompkins, a post-war comic character in films and on radio. He never properly recovered from the trauma of war and took to the bottle in later years, becoming melancholic. After 1917 he only laughed when acting. Like many clowns, he was deeply lachrymose inside and, prone to fits of chronic depression, he took his own life in 1936, dying penniless.

William Stephen Hill, Captain, Staff GHQ, became a successful businessman after inheriting his father's business empire in 1933. After the war he never played cricket seriously again.

Sebastian St John Aloysius Renshaw and Daniel Kingdom Dangerfield III, Captains, 7th Battalion, Middlesex Regiment, were both killed during the attack on Gommecourt on 1 July 1916. Renshaw's body was never found.

Scott Patrick Mackenzie, Captain, 1st Division, Australian and New Zealand Army Corps, saw service in Gallipolli and on the Western Front. After the war he returned to his native country and forged a successful career as a lawyer, playing a few matches for Victoria 2nd XI.

Mansoor Ali 'Jammy' Khan joined the British Army as a liaison officer at Staff HQ, but never saw a shot fired in anger. After the war he returned to India, where he became something of a wastrel, womaniser and nationalist agitator. In his later years becoming extremely fat and died of a heart attack at the age of 47 while servicing one of his concubines.

Horatio Marcus Winston Harvey-Winford, University of Oxford and Essex, Major, Royal London Rifles, survived the war despite being twice gravely wounded. His injuries prevented him playing cricket again, but he became a much-admired career soldier, rising to the rank of Lieutenant General during World War Two. Created Lord Aycliff in 1947, 'Winnie' was renowned as a vociferous fixture in the House of Lords and a successful businessman after leaving the army. He became one of the wealthiest men in England before his death in 1965.

Peregrine Stanley 'Pongo' Smelling, ferocious fast bowler for the University of Oxford and Surrey, Captain, Royal London Rifles, was killed during the third battle of Ypres (historically known as Passchendaele) leading his company through no man's land. Like many who perished in that godforsaken place, his body was never found.

Emily Dickens' prayer was answered: Wilfred Gilbert Harold Fulton, Lieutenant, 10th Battalion (Sportsmen's), Royal London Regiment, recovered from his appalling injuries following pioneering, life-saving surgery. He never played cricket again but kept the battered and bloodied copy of the *Wisden Cricket Almanac* that had saved his life at Gommecourt as a permanent memento of his days as a soldier in the Great War.

Despite the confusion over her sexuality, Emily married Will after the war, and they emigrated to New Zealand where they became sheep farmers. It was not a great physical marriage and there were no children, but they were both able to find some peace of mind.

The belligerent pacifist Calvin Augustus Moseley registered as a conscientious objector at the outbreak of war, but subsequently joined the Royal Army Medical Corps as a stretcher-bearer and was twice decorated for bravery. In 1919 he took up politics and became Labour Member of Parliament for Skegness in 1924 but lost his seat after defecting to the British Communist Party. An early and vociferous critic of the Nazis and other fascist regimes, he renounced pacifism and enlisted in the International Brigade in the Spanish Civil War and was killed in 1938.

His younger brother Roland left school in 1917, lied about his age and enlisted as a private soldier in the Middlesex Regiment. Gung-ho to the end, he was killed in action in November 1918, two days before the end of the war and his own 19th birthday.

After her ignominious dismissal from Wickham Dale, Matron Olive Blackwell's life went rapidly downhill. After some menial jobs, she took to occasional prostitution and even more base depravity. Her health ruined by chronic alcoholism, she succumbed to the influenza pandemic of 1918 and died, penniless and alone, a week after Armistice Day, aged 49. She was not mourned.

Professor Jeremy Brooman proved extraordinarily successful in turning around the fortunes of Wickham Dale College and remained as headmaster until his retirement in 1938. He was one of the most-revered and best-loved of all the school's principals.

James Kennedy Lionel Wright-Herbert, Lieutenant, 10th (Sportsmen's) Battalion, Royal London Regiment, survived his ordeal at Gommecourt, but after returning to duty six months later was gravely wounded again and subsequently invalided out of the services. He inherited the family fortune on the death of his father in 1932, becoming an extraordinarily successful entrepreneur until his own death in 1963. Due to his injuries, he was never able to play cricket again.

After he had dismissed Lieutenant Jack Bigglesworth in the afternoon of 1 July 1916, Frederick Charles Arthur Wright-Herbert, Captain, 10th (Sportsmen's) Battalion, Royal London Regiment, University of Cambridge and Middlesex, a larger-than-life free spirit, was never seen again. It had been hoped that his name may have been included among the prisoners taken that day, but when no confirmation came, he was listed – 'Missing in Action, Presumed Killed'. Following Jack's report to Brigade HQ, attempts were made by the Wright-Herbert family to get Freddie awarded a posthumous Victoria Cross, but they came to nothing, since his actions could not be substantiated. Many years later, a German officer who had taken part in the counterattack to regain the front-line trench at Gommecourt wrote a memoir, mentioning that a severely wounded British officer, alone and manning a machine gun, had kept them at bay for some time before being overwhelmed, but the officer was never identified, and his body never recovered.

So perished the greatest cricketer of his generation, aged just 22, remembered only on the War Graves Commission memorial at Gommecourt Park, as a British soldier with no resting place, and on the Roll of Honour at Wickham Dale College for Boys, for those who gave their lives in the service of king and country.

The survivors all found some level of redemption, but none of the cricketers of Wickham Dale ever saw one another again.

To this day, Wickham Dale remains one of the foremost and respected public schools of England, a place for the sons of the rich and well-to-do to receive a traditional education. Many of its former pupils still advance to become members of parliament, captains of industry and renowned sportsmen. Cricket is still played in the Long Field, where the wicket and facilities are so good that they are often used for Surrey County matches.

But the spirits of 1914 have never been forgotten. Every boy in the school team who played in that final fixture against Christminster in July of that year volunteered to join the colours and serve his country. Of that glorious 11, five paid the ultimate price for their patriotism, three more were gravely wounded and only two played cricket again. It is said that, on a warm, clear summer's night, anyone venturing into the Long Field can see and hear, if they keep their eyes wide and ears to the ground, the ghosts of 1914 – Pongo Smelling hurling thunderbolts at Freddie Wright-Herbert – and the cheery chatter of young boys playing their noble game.

If you listen very quietly – and believe.

# APPENDIX – HISTORICAL NOTES

SOUTH AFRICA V ENGLAND TEST SERIES 1913–14

### 1st Test – Lord's, Durban, 13–17 December 1913

**South Africa 182** (Taylor 109, Barnes 5-57) & **111** (Barnes 5-48, Relf 3-31)

**England 450** (Douglas 119, Hobbs 82, Bird 61, Tennyson 52)

*England won by an innings and 157 runs.*

### 2nd Test – Old Wanderers, Johannesburg 26–30, December 1913

**South Africa 160** (Hartigan 51, Barnes 8-56) & **231** (Nourse 56, Barnes 9-103)

**England 403** (Rhodes 152, Mead 102, Relf 63, Blankenburg 5-83, Newberry 3-93)

*England won by an innings and 12 runs.*

### 3rd Test – Old Wanderers, Johannesburg 1–5 January 1914

**England 238** (Hobbs 92, Taylor 3-15, Blankenburg 3-54) & **308** (Mead 86, Douglas 77, Newberry 4-72, Blankenburg 3-66)

**South Africa 151** (Hearne 5-49, Barnes 3-26) & **304** (Zulch 82, Taylor 70, Barnes 5-102)

*England won by 91 runs.*

### 4th Test – Lord's, Durban 14–18 February 1914

**South Africa 170** (Hands 51, Barnes 7-56, Rhodes 3-33) & **305** (Taylor 93, Barnes 7-88)

**England 163** (Hobbs 64, Carter 6-50) & **154-5** (Hobbs 97, Blankenburg 3-43)

*Match Drawn*

### 5th Test – St George's Park, Port Elizabeth 27 February – 3 March 1914

**South Africa 193** (Hands 83, Douglas 4-14, Woolley 3-71) & **228** (Taylor 87, Zulch 60, Booth 4-49, Bird 3-38)

**England 411** (Mead 117, Woolley 54, Lundie 4-101) & **11-0**

*England won by 10 wickets.*

### *ENGLAND WIN THE SERIES 4-0*

## BATTLE OF GOMMECOURT COMMANDERS

The donkeys who led the lions

British Army Commander-in-Chief – General
(later Field Marshal and 1st Earl Haig)
Sir Douglas Haig, KT, GCB, OM, GCVO, KCIE

British 3rd Army – Lieutenant General Edmund Allenby

VII Corps – Lieutenant General Sir Thomas D'Oyly Snow

46th Division – Major General Edward Stuart-Wortley

56th Division – Major General Charles Amyatt-Hull

Like many of his contemporary generals, Sir Douglas Haig (1861–1928) was a Victorian and Edwardian cavalryman who found it difficult to come to terms with the modern mechanised warfare of 1914–18. He saw service in India, the Sudan and South Africa before being appointed to command the British Expeditionary Force (BEF) 1st Army in 1914, taking over from Sir John French as commander-in-chief in late 1915. He was heir to the Haig & Haig whisky distillery company.

After becoming known as 'Butcher Haig', the man who sacrificed hundreds of thousands of ordinary lives to his policy of attrition, his reputation recovered somewhat after 1918 when, along with Prime Minister David Lloyd-George, he was acknowledged as one of the men most responsible for winning the war, although his portrayals by John Mills in the 1969 film *Oh! What a Lovely War* and Geoffrey Palmer in the TV comedy series *Blackadder Goes Forth* were far from sympathetic – he was represented as an egotistical, uncaring man, synonymous with the carnage and futility of World War One battles. His public funeral in 1928 was declared a day of national mourning.

Edmund Henry Hynman Allenby (1861–1936), later Field Marshal 1st Viscount Allenby GCB, GCMB, GCVO, is perhaps best known for being portrayed by British actor Jack Hawkins in David Lean's 1962 film *Lawrence of Arabia*, based on the adventures of T.E. Lawrence in the Arab revolt and Eastern Campaign against the Ottoman Empire in World War One.

He also had served in South Africa, and in 1914 was appointed to command the Cavalry Brigade of the BEF to Belgium and France. In 1915 he was promoted to the command of the

British 3rd Army in the western theatre and was the commanding officer at the time of Gommecourt, where his orders were to protect the northern flank of the British 4th Army attacking in the Somme valley.

In 1917 he was transferred to the command of the Egyptian Expeditionary Force (EEF) with which he was instrumental in the capture of Jerusalem from the Turks. He was effectively Lawrence's commanding officer during the campaign and was later British High Commissioner for Egypt and the Sudan from 1919 to 1925.

A tall, powerful looking man, he was nicknamed 'The Bull' for his bellowing outbursts of rage and was sarcastically described by one of his colleagues as 'A Thud and Blunder' general.

Lieutenant General Sir Thomas D'Oyly Snow (1858–1940) commanded the British VII Corps, responsible for the attack at Gommecourt. It was often said that he was more afraid of Allenby and Haig than he was of the enemy! He was the grandfather of television presenters Peter and Jon Snow and the great-grandfather of populist TV historian Dan Snow, who is also the great-great-grandson of wartime prime minister David Lloyd-George on his mother's side. From 1917, Lloyd-George was responsible for appointing the generals.

Major General Edward James Montagu-Stuart-Wortley CB, CMG, DSO, MVO (1857–1934), commander 46th Division, carried the can for the failure at Gommecourt after his troops failed miserably to engage the enemy and support the more successful 56th Division. The 46th sustained the fewest casualties of 13 British divisions engaged on 1 July 1916. Haig gave him his marching orders three days later.

The commander of the 56th Division, Major General Charles Patrick Amyatt-Hull CB (1865–1920), was absolved of blame for the disaster and died shortly after the end of the war. His son Richard was a field marshal in World War Two and chief of the defence staff in the 1960s, effectively Britain's top soldier.

\*

The No 15 hand grenade used in the Great War was nicknamed 'cricket ball' due to its round shape. It was much used by the Australian Army in the Gallipoli campaign in 1915, hence its nickname. Although withdrawn in late 1915 due to its instability, the name stuck with reference to all hand grenades.

'Tommy' and 'Blighty' are generic terms used by soldiers in World War One for the simple British (usually English) soldier, and for England or home. 'Tommy' is a shortening of Thomas or Tommy Atkins, a mythical British soldier from the Napoleonic War. 'Blighty' is believed to have derived from the Bengali language. A 'Blighty Wound' was an injury that, although not life-threatening, was serious enough for the recipient to be discharged from the forces and sent home. Both terms probably originated from India or other colonies of the former British Empire.

# FOR UNCLE CHARLIE

HORACE CHARLES RICHARDSON

D COMPANY

1ST BATTALION DEVONSHIRE REGIMENT 9964

95TH BRIGADE

5TH DIVISON

BEF 3RD ARMY (FRANCE AND FLANDERS)

Killed in Action 23 April 1917

Remembered on the Arras Memorial
for soldiers with no known grave

CPSIA information can be obtained
at www.ICGtesting.com
Printed in the USA
LVHW031609160322
713506LV00011B/1111